GEOGRAPHY QUIZ

S. Muthiah is a well-known cartographer. Educated in Sri Lanka, India and the United States, he has spent most of his life as a senior journalist in Ceylon. He has edited *The Social and Economic Atlas of India, An Atlas of India* and *The Road Atlas of India* in addition to several other cartographic publications.

GEOGRAPHY QUIZ

S. MUTHIAH

RUPA

Published by
Rupa Publications India Pvt. Ltd 1992
7/16, Ansari Road, Daryaganj
New Delhi 110002

Sales centres:

Allahabad Bengaluru Chennai
Hyderabad Jaipur Kathmandu
Kolkata Mumbai

ISBN: 978-81-716-7093-2

Seventh impression 2017

10 9 8 7

The moral right of the author has been asserted.

Typeset in 11/12 pts. Garamond by Mindways Design, New Delhi

CONTENTS

PREFACE

Geography has been defined as "the science of the surface of the earth and its inhabitants". It has also been described as "the science of the earth's form, its physical features, climate, population, etc." But to me it has always been a subject which helped me learn about "faraway places with strange sounding names" and the people who lived in them. It also always seemed to add to my knowledge of the old familiar places and those who called them home. In other words, Geography, to me, has always been about thousands of places on earth, the people who live in them and what is special about each of those places that enable people to live in them as they do.

Such a subject, it would seem obvious, is one that every person on earth should have some knowledge about, because it concerns every one of us and our place in the world. Unfortunately, few anywhere in the world consider it a subject of any importance. In fact, in a 1990 US-USSR survey, it was found that in the ten advanced countries surveyed, an adequate geographical knowledge existed only in 70 per cent of those tested in Sweden, and it went down to 45 per cent in the USSR., with the USA, and the UK scoring about 55 per cent. The results for the 18 to 24 age group were only slightly better in the ten countries, going up on the average from 55 per cent to 60 per cent. The situation in India is likely to be far worse, for Geography in this country is a neglected, forgotten subject.

It is in this sad scenario, and in an attempt to get

Geography its due attention, that I decided to work on this book. To me there was no question but that every literate person should have some idea of Geography, about the places where they live, the countries that neighbour them and the other countries in the world. But as I began to frame the questions, I became even more conscious of the variety of Geography. Geography is not merely Physical Geography and Political Geography, but it is also Human Geography, Economic Geography, Social Geography, Historical Geography and a variety of other Geographies, all concerned with the world we live in and what we do in it. With that in mind, I've paid some attention to all of them throughout this work.

It would have been very easy to frame questions under all this variety of heads by just picking names from the whole gamut of atlases and texts available. But I decided that the route to be taken should not be as simple as that, the end result of which might have been a large number of places with strange-sounding names but with little significance to most people reading this book, and more so in the case of those in India. With this in mind, I have attempted to frame questions about places and matters geographic which have some, or should have some, significance to most persons in India and which also have some universal significance.

To ensure greater attention to the more specific, I've divided the book into 12 chapters. The General Geography chapter deals with both geographic terms as well as with aspects of world geography and geographic records. India could have been a chapter by itself, but I've chosen to break the country into four zones in the hope that all who go through this slim volume will be a little more conscious of the different parts of the country. With more and more emphasis being placed by India on its relations with its neighbours, a special chapter is devoted to countries which are our neighbours. That leaves a chapter for the rest of Asia and a chapter each for the five other major continents, Antarctica alone being combined with another continent, Australasia.

To answer most of these questions a good atlas and a dictionary would suffice — and if you choose to go through the questions in that manner, that would still be all right by me, because it would still help increase your geography-consciousness. But a better way would be to try to answer all the questions without turning to the reference books for help. A moderate to good score would, then, be something to be proud of.

The majority of the questions in this book, as I have already said, are about places or areas or physical features of some significance. Even if you know them as answers to the questions, do you know where exactly they are? Every chapter in this book is preceded by a political outline map of the region under scrutiny. As you answer the questions, you might like to locate the respective names on these maps. While attempting this, please note that the use of word "exactly" in some questions refers only to an area located by its direction or a particular state or province or with reference to a physical feature (for example, such a question could be answered with "North-Eastern India" or "Arunachal Pradesh" or "by the Brahmaputra river").

By offering alternatives for each question, I've not only made the challenge a bit easier and, therefore, more interesting, but I've tried to pick the options from as close to the correct answer as possible. This should in some ways quadruple your knowledge of a particular area.

A word about the spellings found in this book. All spellings of Indian names are according to the recommendation of the Survey of India. Spellings of other names are according to George Philip's, one of the world's leading cartographic organisations. It should also be added that this book was compiled before parts of the USSR declared themselves independent and before Yugoslavia began breaking up; when answering questions about these parts of the world, remember this was a world before the 'second revolution'. And when it comes to superlatives, such as the biggest, hottest, etc., there are, sometimes, different answers found in different reference sources and, where this is so, the alternatives are given.

While this is being done to avoid dispute, debate is not the purpose of this slim volume. It is merely a compilation of questions to interest you in Geography through the discovery of "faraway places with strange-sounding names" as well as of "those old familiar places" that often fade from mind. If I've succeeded in evoking that interest, you're bound to have fun with what follows.

Happy voyaging round the world.

Madras ·   S.M.

I

GENERAL GEOGRAPHY

Definitions
Terms
Records

1. What is peninsula?

   (a) A narrow bit of land (b) A mountainous island (c) A piece of land surrounded by water on three sides (d) A range of hills

2. In which direction is the Tropic of Capricorn in relation to the Equator?

   (a) North (b) South (c) East (d) West

3. Which is the largest ocean?

   (a) Indian (b) Pacific (c) Atlantic (d) Arctic

4. What does a barometer indicate?

   (a) Changes in atmospheric (air) pressure (b) Changes in temperature (c) The amount of rainfall (d) The direction of the winds

5. What is the difference between a gulf and a bay?

   (a) A gulf is big and a bay is small (b) A gulf is at a rivermouth and a bay is not (c) A bay is surrounded by cliffs, a gulf by lowland (d) Both are part of the sea that extend considerably into the land, but a bay usually has a wider entrance than a gulf.

6. Which continent is in its entirety further north of the Equator?

   (a) Asia (b) Europe (c) North America (d) Africa

7. What do isotherms indicate?

   (a) The height in particular areas (b) The rainfall in certain areas (c) The temperatures in particular areas (d) The snowfall in some areas

8. What do you call a narrow neck of land that connects two larger landmasses?

(a) Peninsula (b) Isthmus (c) Cape (d) Strait

9. How is density of population usually measured?

(a) Persons per sq. km. (b) The number of people in a country (c) The number of households in a country (d) The number of births from one census to the next in a country.

10. Which water body surrounds the North Pole?

(a) Atlantic Ocean (b) Pacific Ocean (c) Indian Ocean (d) Arctic Ocean

11. Approximately when does the South-West Monsoon begin in India?

(a) Late April (b) October (c) Early June (d) January

12. What is the name given to the widened rivermouth found at the point a river enters the sea?

(a) Estuary (b) Bay (c) Gulf (d) Delta

13. What do isobars indicate?

(a) The atmospheric pressure in a particular area (b) Rainfall in different places (c) Wind strengths in several areas (d) Places with the same temperature

14. What is significant about the town of Greenwich?

(a) The International Date Line passes through it (b) The 0° (Zero) meridian passes through it and therefore the world sets its time by it (c) It is at 180° longitude (d) It is a major horological research centre in Britain

15. What is the triangular landmass that forms at its mouth when a river splits into several branches just before entering the sea?

(a) Cape (b) Island (c) Estuary (d) Delta

16. From west to east, what are the three main island groups in the Pacific called?

(a) Melanesia, Micronesia and Polynesia
(b) Polynesia, Micronesia and Melanesia
(c) Melanesia, Polynesia and Micronesia
(d) Micronesia, Polynesia and Melanesia

17. What is a typhoon called in the Atlantic?

(a) A typhoon (b) A cyclone (c) A hurricane
(d) A tornado

18. What meridian is the International Date Line?

(a) The 180° meridian (b) The 0° meridian
(c) The 90° meridian (d) The 135° meridian

19. What is a narrow waterway separating two bits of land called?

(a) A bay (b) A gulf (c) A strait (d) An isthmus

20. Which three continents have the largest areas of coniferous forest?

(a) Australia, Europe and South America
(b) Asia, North America and Europe (c) North America, South America and Europe (d) Asia, Australia and South America

21. What is the geographical term for "land's end", that tip of land which projects into the sea?

(a) A headland (b) A spit (c) A peninsula
(d) A cape

22. Outside the Mediterranean region, where else is a Mediterranean climate found?

(a) The Japanese and Chinese coasts (b) The southern coast of Australia and parts of the western coast of North and South America (c) The east coast of North America (d) The North Atlantic coast of Africa

23. What is a more precise geographical name for a tableland?

(a) A hill (b) A headland (c) A plateau (d) A mountain

24. Which continent has the largest area of Equatorial Rain Forest?

(a) Africa (b) South America (c) Asia (d) Australia

25. Where is the greatest ocean depth found?

(a) In the Atlantic (b) In the Dead Sea (c) In the Indian Ocean (d) The Mariana Trench in the Pacific Ocean

26. What are those smaller rivers that flow into a large, main river called?

(a) Feeders (b) Streams (c) Tributaries (d) Rivulets

27. In which part of the world would you find the Veld?

(a) Argentina (b) Australia (c) Central Europe (d) South Africa

28. What do Mauna Loa, Krakatoa and Stromboli have in common?

(a) All are volcanoes (b) All are mountains (c) All are in Italy (d) All are islands

29. What is the difference between a lake and a tank?

(a) A lake is small and a tank is big (b) A lake has flowing water, a tank has still water (c) A

lake is a geographical feature, a tank is not
(d) Both are land-enclosed water bodies, but
the latter is manmade

30. How many degrees north and south are the
Tropics?

(a) 47 degrees (b) 23.5 degrees (c) 12
degrees (d) 30 degrees

31. What is a water-surrounded bit of land called?

(a) An island (b) A peninsula (c) A cape (d) A
spit

32. The earth is not a true sphere. Then what is
it?

(a) It is elliptical (b) It is oval (c) It is slightly
flattened at the Poles and bulges slightly at the
Equator (d) It is flat at the top and bottom

33. What is a prairie?

(a) A scrub forest in North America (b) A
North American farmland (c) A kind of
American vegetation (d) A large, flat grassland
in North America

34. What is the science of making maps called?

(a) Cartography (b) Seismography (c) Pantog-
raphy (d) Geodesy

35. When a high area of land drops steeply,
especially into the sea, what is the land
formation that results called?

(a) Valley (b) Cliff (c) Plain (d) Precipice

36. What is the approximate Russian equivalent of
the prairie?

(a) Siberian plain (b) Taiga (c) Tundra
(d) Steppes

37. Excluding Australia, generally treated as a continent, which is the largest island in the world?

(a) Greenland (b) Madagascar (c) Hispaniola (d) Britain

38. In what units is rainfall usually measured in India?

(a) Cubic centimetres (b) Centimetres (c) Grams (d) Litres

39. What is the Gulf Stream?

(a) A river in North America (b) A wind in the Caribbean (c) A warm sea current from the Gulf of Mexico (d) The entrance to a gulf in North America.

40. What is the largest gorge in the world?

(a) Grand Canyon, USA, (b) Death Valley (c) Kashmir Valley (d) Marble Rocks

41. How did the Atlantic get its name?

(a) From Atlanta in the USA (b) From the lost continent Atlantis (c) From the word "atlas" (d) From the Atlas Mountains in North Africa

42. These "rivers of ice" are always slowly on the move. What is their correct name?

(a) Ice packs (b) Snowcaps (c) Icefloes (d) Glaciers

43. Which continent doesn't have a permanent population?

(a) South America (b) Africa (c) Australasia (d) Antarctica

44. What is the approximate African equivalent of the prairie?

(a) Steppes (b) Savannah (c) Veld (d) Pampas

45. How many principal planets are there in the Solar System?

(a) Nine (b) Twelve (c) Ten (d) Seven

46. What colour is laterite soil?

(a) Brown (b) Yellow (c) Red (d) Pink

47. What is the temperature of the sun estimated at approximately?

(a) 5000 degrees F (b) 6000 degrees F (c) 7000 degrees F (d) 212 degrees F

48. What is another name for the "Cold Deserts" of the world?

(a) Tundra (b) Taiga (c) Glacier (d) Snow-field

49. How are alluvial plains formed?

(a) By rivers depositing their sand and silt on the land during floods (b) By the snow melting and moistening the soil (c) By heavy rains making the soil marshy (d) By winds depositing a fine sand on the plains

50. What is the time difference for every degree of longitude?

(a) Eight minutes (b) Ten minutes (c) Four minutes (d) Twelve minutes

51. If the water surrounding the land man lives on is called the hydrosphere, what is the rocky crust of the earth on which we live called?

(a) Atmosphere (b) Stratosphere (c) Barysphere (d) Lithosphere

52. What do contours on maps indicate?

(a) The temperature in different areas (b) Heights of land above the sea level (c) The vegetation in different areas (d) The different kinds of soil

53. Where would you find the Trade Winds?

(a) Between the Tropics and blowing towards the Equator, (b) In the Atlantic Ocean (c) By the Cape of Good Hope (d) Blowing across Europe

54. The surface of the earth is about 500 million sq. km. About how much of this is water?

(a) 50 per cent (b) 90 per cent (c) 70 per cent (d) 30 per cent

55. What is the latitude of the Arctic Circle?

(a) 80 degrees North (b) 66.5 degrees South (c) 80 degrees South (d) 66.5 degrees North

56. What is the upper part of the atmosphere called?

(a) Lithosphere (b) Stratosphere (c) Barysphere (d) Hydrosphere

57. What does the scale 1: 1,000,000 represent in linear measure?

(a) 1 cm = 10 km (b) 1 m = 1 mile (c) 1" = $6\frac{1}{2}$ miles (d) 1 cm = 1 km

58. Which part of the earth is the South Temperate Zone?

(a) Between the Equator and the Tropic of Capricorn (b) Between the Tropic of Capricorn and the Antarctic Circle (c) Between the Equator and the Antarctic Circle (d) Between the two Tropics

59. What have Humboldt, Benguela and Kuro Siwo in common?

(a) All are ocean currents (b) All are African cities (c) All are great explorers (d) All are mountain peaks

60. In which part of the world would you find cyclones?

(a) In the China Seas (b) In the Caribbean (c) The Indian Ocean and its littoral (d) By the Cape of Good Hope

61. What is loess?

(a) A kind of alluvial soil (b) The fine sand found in the desert (c) The sand the Mediterranean winds blow up (d) A fine dust that covers the land in interior China

62. What is sometimes referred to as the World Ocean?

(a) All the oceans of the world when considered as one ocean because they are interconnected (b) The Pacific Ocean (c) The Atlantic Ocean (d) The ocean south of the African mainland

63. What are the Selvas?

(a) The forests in the Tropics (b) Hot, wet equatorial evergreen forests (c) The jungles of India (d) The woods in the Iberian peninsula

64. What are the Roaring Forties?

(a) A typhoon in the China Sea (b) A hurricane in the Caribbean (c) A kind of tornado (d) Strong winds that blow between 40 and 50 degrees South, in a direction opposite to the winds

65. What happens in land that is in the rain shadow?

(a) It gets no rain, because the rains are cut off by high mountains at one edge of the land (b) It gets very heavy rain during most of the year (c) The skies above are always cloudy (d) The winds blow much less in these parts

66. What is the Continental Shelf?

(a) A plateau in the centre of a continent (b) The land that gently slopes and extends below sea level from the coasts of the continents before sharply sloping to form the seafloor in the deeps (c) Mountain ranges that edge a continent (d) The raised land on a continent's edge

67. What is the more common name for the winds that are sometimes called the Anti-trades?

(a) Cyclones (b) The North Winds (c) The East Winds (d) The Westerlies

68. What is a Cash Crop?

(a) A rich harvest (b) A crop that is not a food crop; it is grown for sale to manufacturers who convert it into products (c) Crops grown in plantations (d) A crop which earns a lot of money

69. What have the Sirocco, Fohn and Mistral in common?

(a) All are Mediterranean towns (b) All are European mountain ranges (c) All are Mediterranean currents (d) All are strong winds, the effect of local conditions

70. Which part of the world is regularly visited by tornadoes?

(a) South-east USA (b) The Caribbean (c) Central America (d) The desert states of the USA

71. What is stock farming?

(a) Plantation activity (b) Farming for the family (c) Cattle-rearing (d) Raising cash crops

72. How are heights of land expressed?

(a) In miles (b) In inches (c) In kilometres
(d) In feet or metres above the sea level

73. Which is the most densely populated continent?

    (a) Europe (b) Asia (c) North America
    (d) Africa

74. Which is the busiest ocean of the world in normal times?

    (a) Pacific (b) Atlantic (c) Indian (d) Arctic

75. What is the Earth's satellite?

    (a) Uranus (b) Neptune (c) Venus (d) Moon

76. What is the hottest place on earth?

    (a) Dalol, Danakil Depression, Ethiopia/Al Aziziyah, Libya (b) Alice Springs, Australia (c) Jaisalmer, India (d) Timbuktoo, Mali

77. Which expedition was the first to sail round the world and conclusively prove that the Earth is round?

    (a) Sir Francis Drake's (b) Vasco da Gama's (c) Christopher Columbus's (d) Magellan's *Victoria*

78. Outside Antarctica, which is the deepest part of the earth?

    (a) The Dead Sea (b) The Aral Sea (c) The Caspian Sea (d) Lake Baikal

79. How many times does the Earth move round the Sun in a year?

    (a) 1.1 times (b) Once (c) 1.25 times
    (d) Twice

80. What do the USSR, China, Brazil, India, and the USA have in common?

    (a) All democracies (b) All have heavy rainfall (c) They are the five most populous countries

(d) All have capitals beginning with the letter 'B'

81. What happens when ships cross the International Date Line?

(a) They have to pay a tax (b) Ships going west from the USA lose a day, ships going east from Japan and Australia gain a day (c) They have to report at the customs post (d) They have to check their clocks against Greenwich Mean Time

82. What is the smallest planet?

(a) Mercury (b) Venus (c) Pluto (d) Mars

83. What is the specific feature of the Mercator Projection?

(a) It distorts the shape of India (b) It flattens the world (c) It makes Australia rectangular (d) It exaggerates Greenland almost 25 times

84. How many satellites does the largest planet have?

(a) Twelve (b) Ten (c) Six (d) Nine (around Jupiter)

85. What is the distance around the Earth at the Equator?

(a) 21,000 km (b) 16,800 km (c) 18,600 km (d) 12,500 km

86. Four of the five most populous countries are also among the five largest countries in the world by area. Which is the fifth largest by area?

(a) Australia (b) Mongolia (c) Zaire (d) Canada

87. From which language is the word "Monsoon" derived?

(a) Arabic (b) Hindi (c) Malayalam (d) Marathi ("Mausim" season)

88. Who or what are Mollweide, Bonne and Gall?

(a) All are explorers (b) All are map projections (c) All are geologists (d) All are editors of atlases

89. What are the Doldrums?

(a) The Trade Winds (b) Areas of great humidity (c) A low-pressure belt round the Equator where there are very light winds and calm seas (d) Areas where the seas are calm

90. What is an oasis and where would you find it?

(a) A small area of green and water in a desert (b) A rich farmland in Asia (c) A desert island in the Pacific (d) A waterhole in the jungle

91. When is the Summer Solstice?

(a) July 23 (b) June 21 (c) May 20 (d) April 13

92. Where is the Torrid Zone?

(a) On either side of the Tropics (b) Between the Arctic and Antarctic Circles (c) On either side of the Equator, up to the Tropics (d) Along the Equator

93. What are permeable rocks?

(a) They soak up water (b) They are oil-bearing rocks (c) They are porous rocks (d) They allow water to pass through them easily

94. Which ocean surrounds Antarctica?

(a) Indian Ocean (b) Southern Ocean (c) Pacific Ocean (d) Atlantic Ocean

95. When is the Vernal Equinox?

(a) December 25 (b) March 21 (c) February 28 (d) January 14

96. What are those unique "pillar" formations found in limestone caves?

(a) Satellites (b) Pillar Rocks (c) Stalactites, from the roofs, and stalagmites, rising from the floor (d) Stratified rocks

97. What is another name for a Highland climate?

(a) A Himalayan climate (b) A Scottish climate (c) A Hill climate (d) An Alpine climate

98. What common feature do Intermontane, Piedmont, and Continental describe?

(a) Types of plateaus (b) Types of soils (c) Types of rocks (d) Types of weather

99. What happens during the equinoxes?

(a) The countries along the Equator are in darkness (b) The countries along the Equator are at their hottest (c) The countries along the Equator are at their wettest (d) The sun shines vertically over the Equator

100. What are Chernozem soils?

(a) Black soils of great fertility — as in the Steppes (b) Infertile soils (c) Soils affected by radiation (d) Soils found in Eastern Europe

II

NORTH INDIA

Jammu and Kashmir
Himachal Pradesh
Chandigarh
Punjab
Haryana
Delhi
Uttar Pradesh
Rajasthan

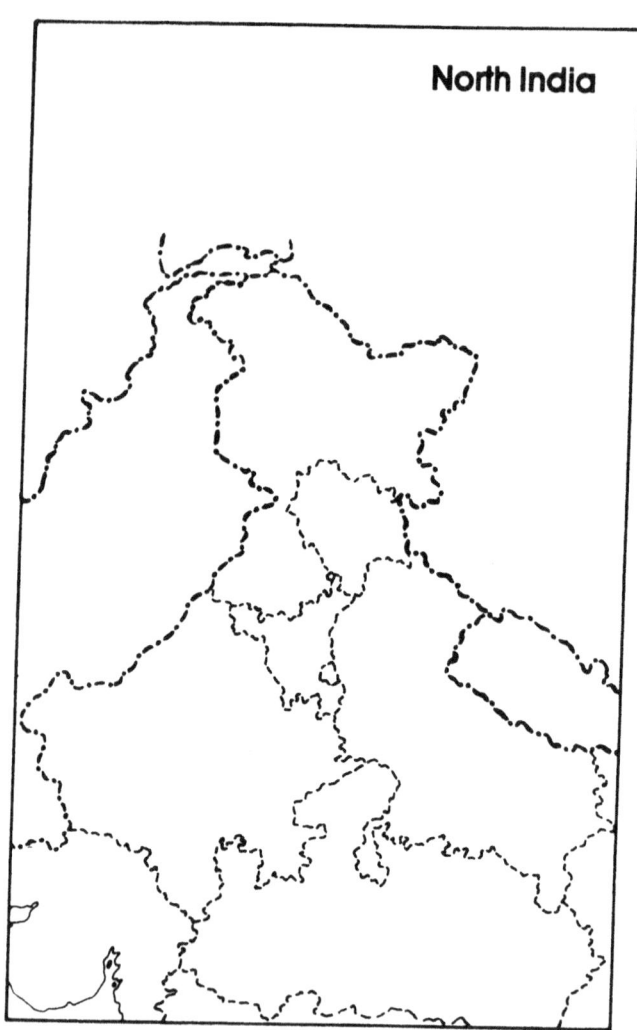

North India

101. What mountain range overlooks Jaipur?

(a) The Vindhyas (b) The Aravallis (c) The Satpuras (d) The Mahadeo Hills

102. What is the last Indian railway station before crossing into Pakistan on the Amritsar-Lahore line?

(a) Atari (b) Ferozpur (c) Fazilka (d) Pathankot

103. On what river is Lucknow?

(a) Ganga (b) Ghaghra (c) Gomati (d) Sarda

104. Where are large deposits of salt to be found in Rajasthan?

(a) Great Indian Desert (b) Aravallis (c) The banks of the Luni (d) The Sambhar Salt Lake

105. What is the chief town of the Kumaon?

(a) Ranikhet (b) Almora (c) Landsdowne (d) Naini Tal

106. Which river forms part of the boundary between Rajasthan and Madhya Pradesh?

(a) Banas (b) Mahi (c) Chambal (d) Luni

107. At what major junction in U.P. do trains from Agra, Bhopal and Kanpur meet?

(a) Jhansi (b) Lucknow (c) Allahabad (d) Etawah

108. Where exactly is Aksai Chin?

(a) Near Leh (b) The north-east corner of Jammu & Kashmir (c) Along the Zaskar mountains (d) South of the Siachen Glacier

109. Does the Son flow through UP? If so, through which part of the State?

(a) Yes, along the Nepal border (b) No, it only flows through Bihar (c) Yes, the south-east corner (d) No, it flows only through Madhya Pradesh

110. What is Jammu & Kashmir's best-known wildlife sanctuary?

(a) Gulmarg (b) Ladakh (c) Nanga Parbat (d) Dachigam

111. Through which districts does the Indira Gandhi Canal flow?

(a) Ganganagar, Bikaner, and Jaisalmer (b) Barmer, Jodhpur, and Nagaur (c) Jhunjhunun, Jaipur, and Ajmer (d) Tonk, Bundi, and Kota

112. In which state is the Kangra Valley?

(a) Haryana (b) Himachal Pradesh (c) Punjab (d) Jammu and Kashmir

113. Of which city could Faridabad, Gurgaon, and Ghaziabad be considered satellite towns?

(a) Aligarh (b) Agra (c) Chandigarh (d) Delhi

114. Which of these rivers does not flow through the Punjab?

(a) Beas (b) Chenab (c) Satluj (d) Ravi

115. Which of these pilgrim centres is the furthest north?

(a) Gangotri (b) Kedarnath (c) Joshimath (d) Badrinath

116. Which of these states has a border with Pakistan?

(a) Uttar Pradesh (b) Punjab (c) Haryana (d) Himachal Pradesh

117. What is the northernmost part of Jammu and Kashmir called?

(a) Shinaki (b) Ladakh (c) Gilgit and Hunza (d) Baltistan

118. Where is the Bhakra Dam?

    (a) Himachal Pradesh (b) Jammu and Kashmir (c) Haryana (d) Punjab

119. Near which holiday resort is the Wular Lake?

    (a) Gulmarg (b) Pahalgam (c) Sonamarg (d) Leh

120. Which is the last major railway junction in the Punjab before Jammu and Kashmir?

    (a) Amritsar (b) Pathankot (c) Jalandhar (d) Gurdaspur

121. In which state is the former princely state of Pataudi?

    (a) Haryana (b) Punjab (c) Himachal Pradesh (d) Uttar Pradesh

122. In which state is Nanda Devi the highest peak?

    (a) Jammu and Kashmir (b) Himachal Pradesh (c) Uttar Pradesh (d) Punjab

123. Which is the longest river in Rajasthan?

    (a) Chambal (b) Mahi (c) Banas (d) Luni

124. What is another name for the Great Indian Desert?

    (a) Thar Desert (b) Rajasthan Desert (c) Bikaner Desert (d) Western Desert

125. Between which mountain ranges does Leh lie?

    (a) Deosai and Karakoram (b) Siwaliks and Pir Panjal (c) Zaskar and Ladakh (d) Pir Panjal and Zaskar

126. What is Keylang the entrance to?

(a) The Doon Valley (b) The Lahul and Spiti region of Himachal Pradesh (c) The Kashmir Valley (d) The Kulu Valley

127. On which river is Delhi?

(a) Ganga (b) Chambal (c) Yamuna (d) Alaknanda

128. For what cultivation is Kotgarh famous?

(a) Apples (b) Pears (c) Grapes (d) Peaches

129. Where does the Survey of India have its headquarters?

(a) Delhi (b) Dehra Dun (c) Roorkee (d) Bareilly

130. Where is there said to be the highest cricket ground in the world?

(a) Naini Tal in Uttar Pradesh (b) Srinagar in Jammu and Kashmir (c) Chail in Himachal Pradesh (d) Dehra Dun in Uttar Pradesh

131. Which is the famous Buddhist pilgrim centre near Varanasi?

(a) Saranath (b) Sanchi (c) Rajgir (d) Bodh Gaya

132. What is the exact political status of Chandigarh?

(a) It is the capital of Haryana (b) It is the capital of the Punjab (c) It is a Union Territory (d) It is a Union Territory where the administrative headquarters of Chandigarh, Punjab and Haryana are situated

133. What is Pantnagar famous for?

(a) It is the home of the Pant family (b) It is an agricultural university and research centre (c) It is a pilgrim centre (d) It is an industrial city

134. What is the major mountain range in northern Ladakh?

(a) Karakoram Range (b) Zaskar Range (c) Pir Panjal Range (d) Great Himalaya

135. What is the name of the "ghost town", once a great capital, that is near Agra?

(a) Sikandra (b) Firozabad (c) Brindavan (d) Fatehpur Sikri

136. In which city is the famous Dal Lake?

(a) Jammu (b) Gulmarg (c) Srinagar (d) Pahalgam

137. Which is the "Sports Goods Capital" of India?

(a) Jalandhar (b) Ludhiana (c) Amritsar (d) Patiala

138. Of which state is Mewar a part?

(a) Jammu and Kashmir (b) Uttar Pradesh (c) Haryana (d) Rajasthan

139. Four of the seven sacred cities of the Hindus — Ayodhya, Haridwar, Mathura and Varanasi — are in one state. Which state?

(a) Rajasthan (b) Uttar Pradesh (c) Haryana (d) Jammu and Kashmir

140. Which is the best-known bird sanctuary in Haryana?

(a) Sultanpur (b) Bharatpur (c) Rajaji (d) Sariska

141. Which is claimed to be the coldest place in Asia?

(a) Gilgit (b) Leh (c) Dras (d) Kargil

142. Which is the biggest hosiery-manufacturing centre in North India?

(a) Jalandhar (b) Hoshiarpur (c) Ambala (d) Ludhiana

143. Near which scenic glacier is the Amarnath Cave?

(a) Kolahoi Glacier (b) Siachen Glacier (c) Nunkun Glacier (d) Zaskar Glacier

144. Which major railway junction and once princely capital is now a major industrial city in south-east Rajasthan?

(a) Kota (b) Tonk (c) Udaipur (d) Bundi

145. What is the base camp for Vaishnodevi?

(a) Srinagar (b) Katra (c) Jammu (d) Gulmarg

146. From where does the "toy train" to Shimla start?

(a) Solan (b) Kasauli (c) Chandigarh (d) Kalka

147. What is the starting point for the trek to the Valley of Flowers?

(a) Chamoli (b) Govindhat (c) Almora (d) Joshimath

148. Where are Shimla's major ski slopes?

(a) Kufri (b) Kulu (c) Manali (d) Kangra

149. Where is the largest manmade lake in Asia?

(a) Govind Sagar, HP (b) Wular Lake, J & K (c) Jai Samand, Rajasthan (d) Naini Tal Lake, UP

150. What do Landsdowne, Chakrata, and Ranikhet have in common?

(a) All are apple-growing centres (b) All have national research institutes (c) All are cantonments (d) All are small hill stations in UP

III

SOUTH INDIA

Andaman and Nicobar Islands
Andhra Pradesh
Tamil Nadu
Pondicherry
Kerala
Karnataka
Lakshadweep

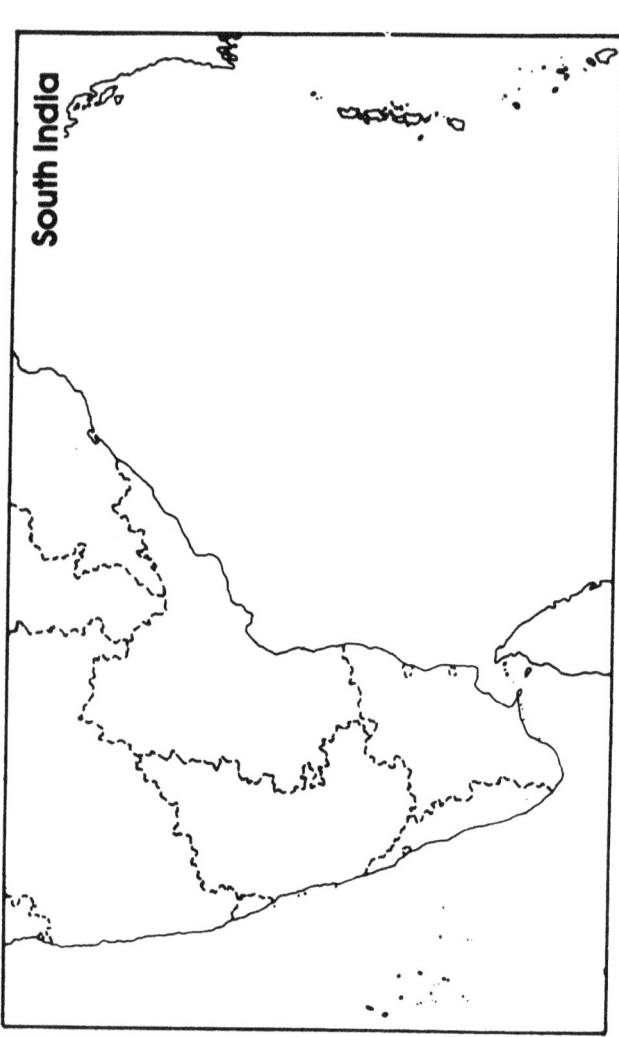

South India

151. In what hills is the small hill station of Yercaud?

(a) Javadi Hills (b) Shevaroy Hills (c) Nilgiris (d) Elagiris

152. To visit which tourist destination would Hassan be used as a base?

(a) Halebid-Belur (b) Bijapur (c) Shravanabelgola (d) Brindavan Gardens

153. Which is the "Lake District" of Andhra Pradesh?

(a) Nizamabad (b) Eluru (c) Warangal (d) Guntur

154. Which part of Pondicherry is an enclave in Kerala?

(a) Vilianur (b) Karaikal (c) Yanam (d) Mahé

155. Where exactly would you expect to find the Borra Caves?

(a) Near Adilabad (b) North-eastern Andhra Pradesh (c) Near Warangal (d) On the Andhra-Orissa border

156. Which waterway runs through much of Andhra Pradesh and ends in northern Tamil Nadu?

(a) The Buckingham Canal (b) Pennar (c) Telugu Ganga (d) Krishna river

157. Which is Cochin's twin city?

(a) Alleppey (b) Mattancheri (c) Alwaye (d) Ernakulam

158. Which island groups are separated by the Ten Degree Channel?

(a) Lakshadweep and Minicoy (b) South Andaman and Little Andaman (c) The Andaman and Nicobar Islands (d) Pamban and Mannar

159. Near which water body is Hospet?

(a) Krishnarajasagar (b) Jog Falls (c) Stanley Reservoir (d) Tungabhadra Reservoir

160. What is Kodungallur better known as, especially in works of history?

(a) Cranganore (b) Calicut (c) Cannanore (d) Cochin (earlier, Musiris)

161. Which is the fourth town in northern Karnataka which forms this important tourist circuit: Aivalli, Badami and Bijapur?

(a) Belgaum (b) Pattadakhal (c) Talikota (d) Bidar

162. Where are the largest and deepest mines?

(a) Hoskote (b) Bellary (c) Anantapur (d) Kolar Gold Fields

163. What do Vellore and Gingee have in common?

(a) Major hospitals (b) Rock forts (c) Large, derelict forts (d) Temple towns

164. With which heavy industry is Bhadravati associated?

(a) Iron (b) Mica (c) Aluminium (d) Heavy Engineering

165. Kodikkarai is on the Coromandel Coast. On which coast is Kilakkarai?

(a) The Malabar Coast (b) The Fisheries Coast (c) The Konkan Coast (d) The Northern Circars

166. Which is the chief town of the Andhra Pradesh "rice bowl"?

(a) Madanapalle (b) Chittoor (c) Nellore (d) Tirupati

167. Which is the chief hill station in the Palani Hills?

38

(a) Kotagiri (b) Coonoor (c) Munnar
(d) Kodaikanal

168. Which was once considered one of the world's most important diamond mining centres?

(a) Golconda (b) Kolar (c) Sandur (d) Cuddappah

169. Which is the major port in southern Tamil Nadu?

(a) Kanniyakumari (b) Tuticorin (c) Tondi
(d) Nagappattinam

170. Which bird sanctuary is near Mysore?

(a) Bandipur (b) Mudumalai (c) Wynaad
(d) Ranganathittoo

171. By which riverbank is Vijayawada?

(a) Krishna (b) Godavari (c) Pennar (d) Tungabhadra

172. What natural feature separates Pamban Island and Mannar Island?

(a) Palk Strait (b) Gulf of Mannar (c) Adam's Bridge (d) Kachativu

173. Which is the major tea-producing centre in the Cardamom Hills?

(a) Anaimudi (b) Munnar (c) Kodaikanal
(d) Valparai

174. Which is the southernmost island in Lakshadweep?

(a) Kalpeni (b) Kavaratti (c) Pitti (d) Minicoy

175. Where is mainland India's Land's End?

(a) Dhanushkodi (b) Cape Comorin (c) Nagercoil (d) Tuticorin

176. What are the Northern Circars?

(a) The north-eastern coast of Andhra Pradesh (and its districts) (b) Andhra Pradesh coastal districts (c) Northern Andhra Pradesh (d) The Godavari and Krishna Deltas

177. Which states does the Palghat Gap connect?

(a) Kerala and Karnataka (b) Tamil Nadu and Karnataka (c) Kerala and Tamil Nadu (d) Tamil Nadu and Andhra Pradesh

178. Where and what is Bitra Island?

(a) A holiday resort in Lakshadweep (b) The main fishing centre in Lakshadweep (c) A lighthouse island in Lakshadweep (d) A bird sanctuary in Lakshadweep

179. A bay and a strait separate India and Sri Lanka. What common name do they have?

(a) Adam (b) Palk (c) Mannar (d) Coromandel

180. What is special about Anaimudi?

(a) It is the highest peak in South India (b) It has a large elephant population (c) It has several tea plantations (d) It is a pass between Kerala and Tamil Nadu

181. Which dam site is near the Stanley Reservoir?

(a) Krishnarajasagar (b) Mettur (c) Grand Anaicut (d) Nagarjunasagar

182. Which wildlife sanctuary is contiguous with Mudumalai and Wynad?

(a) Nagarhole (b) Periyar (c) Bandipur (d) Anamalai

183. From Tirupati in the foothills towards which famed pilgrim centre in the hills do pilgrims head?

(a) Tiruvannamalai (b) Sri Kalahasti (c) Chamundi (d) Thirumalai

184. When the Kaveri river drops as soon as it enters Tamil Nadu, what waterfalls does it create?

(a) Jog Falls (b) Five Falls, Courtallam, (c) Hogenakkal Falls (d) Sivasamudram Falls

185. A portion of which Karnataka district is almost an enclave in Andhra Pradesh?

(a) Tumkur (b) Kolar (c) Bellary (d) Raichur

186. Near which capital is Ross Island, an area protected for its natural and historical wealth?

(a) Madras (b) Port Blair (c) Trivandrum (d) Kavaratti

187. Which is Bangalore's "hill station"?

(a) Horsley Hills (b) Shevaroy Hills (c) Madikeri (d) Nandi Hills

188. From near which major town does the Godavari Delta begin to spread?

(a) Rajahmundry (b) Vijayawada (c) Guntur (d) Machilipatnam

189. Of which waterbody is the Vembanad Lake a part?

(a) Cochin Harbour (b) Periyar River (c) The Alleppey backwaters (d) Ashtamudi Lake

190. What was Kollidam once called?

(a) Grand Anaicut (b) Coleroon (c) Srirangam Island (d) Lower Anaicut

191. In which state is Karwar being developed as an important port?

(a) Andhra Pradesh (b) Tamil Nadu (c) Kerala (d) Karnataka

192. On which river is Madurai?

(a) Vaigai (b) Kaveri (c) Palar (d) Tamaraparani

193. Where is ship-building a major industry on the Coromandel coasts?

(a) Madras (b) Pondicherry (c) Vishakhapatnam (d) Cuddalore

194. Which lake is part of the Thekkady wildlife sanctuary?

(a) Ashtamudi (b) Periyar (c) Kayankulam (d) Vembanad

195. Which is the southernmost point on India-owned territory?

(a) Indira Point (b) Cape Comorin (c) Dhanushkodi (d) Point Calimere

·96. Which are the best-known waterfalls in Karnataka?

(a) Sivasamudram (b) Hogenakkal (c) Jog (d) Talaicauvery

197. Near which capital city is the Kovalam beach resort?

(a) Kavaratti (b) Pondicherry (c) Madras (d) Trivandrum

198. Which lake is partly in Andhra Pradesh and partly in Tamil Nadu?

(a) Stanley Reservoir (b) Pulicat Lake (c) Tungabhadra Reservoir (d) Nagarjunasagar

199. What is Madikeri better known as?

(a) Mangalore (b) Mandya (c) Mysore (d) Mercara

200. From where does Mangalore port get most of the iron ore it exports?

(a) Kudremukh (b) Bhadravathi (c) Hosdurga (d) Tumkur

IV

EAST INDIA

Arunachal Pradesh
Nagaland
Manipur
Mizoram
Tripura
Assam
Meghalaya
Sikkim
West Bengal
Bihar
Orissa

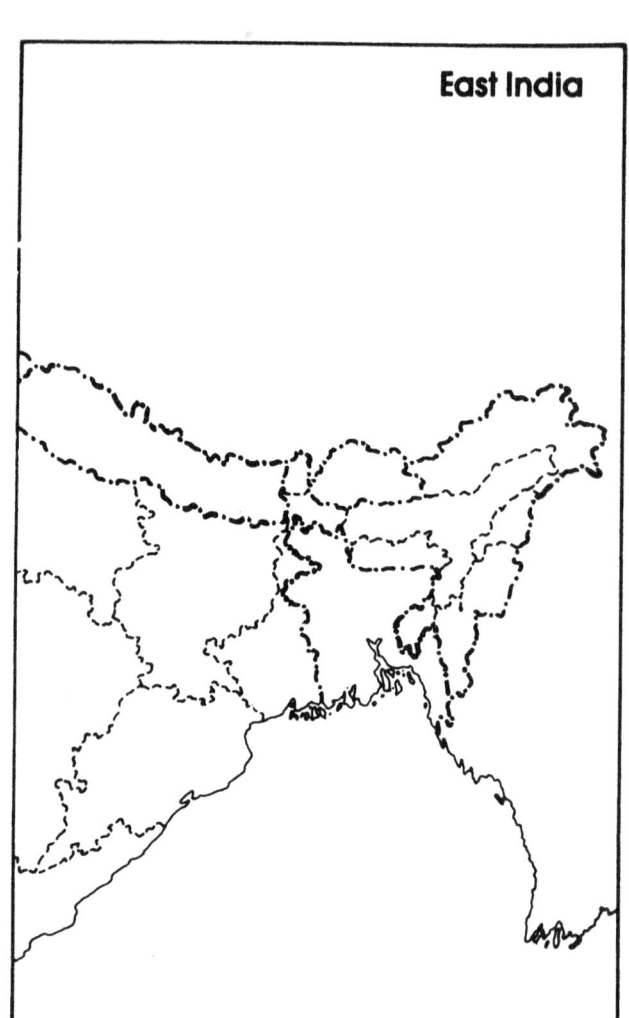

East India

201. With which wildlife sanctuary is the one-horned rhinoceros specially associated?

(a) Manas (b) Keibul Lamjao (c) Kaziranga (d) Orang

202. In which state is Bodh Gaya?

(a) Bihar (b) Orissa (c) West Bengal (d) Sikkim

203. Where is there a major steel plant in Orissa?

(a) Cuttack (b) Paradwip (c) Hirakud (d) Raurkela

204. What state is virtually sandwiched between Bangladesh and Myanmar?

(a) Tripura (b) Mizoram (c) Manipur (d) Nagaland

205. Which is the easternmost state or Union Territory in India?

(a) Assam (b) Arunachal Pradesh (c) Nagaland (d) Manipur

206. Which major port has been developed in Orissa in recent years?

(a) Konarak (b) Ganjam (c) Paradwip (d) Puri

207. Where is there a major state-owned steel plant in Bihar?

(a) Dhanbad (b) Jamshedpur (c) Chittaranjan (d) Bokaro

208. Which is the biggest dam site and reservoir in Orissa?

(a) Hirakud (b) Chilika (c) Cuttack (d) Raurkela

209. In which states will you find the Duars?

(a) West Bengal and Sikkim (b) Assam and Meghalaya (c) West Bengal and Assam (d) Assam and Arunachal Pradesh

210. Which state is bounded by Bangladesh on three sides?

(a) Mizoram (b) Meghalaya (c) West Bengal (d) Tripura

211. Which is claimed by many to be the wettest place on earth?

(a) Cherrapunji (b) Shillong (c) Tura (d) Jowai

212. Which river in West Bengal has a major hydroelectric power and irrigation scheme associated with it?

(a) Bhagirathi (b) Damodar (c) Hughli (d) Tista

213. Which state/states in this region have borders with China?

(a) Sikkim and Assam (b) Nagaland and Manipur (c) Sikkim and Arunachal Pradesh (d) Assam and West Bengal

214. What is the capital of Assam?

(a) Guwahati (b) Dispur (c) Jorhat (d) Tezpur

215. By the border of which Indian state is Kanchenjunga?

(a) Sikkim (b) West Bengal (c) Assam (d) Arunachal Pradesh

216. Which Indian state in its east-west entirety does the Brahmaputra traverse?

(a) Arunachal Pradesh (b) West Bengal (c) Meghalaya (d) Assam

217. Which is the hill region of Meghalaya?

(a) Khasi-Jaintia Hills (b) Lushai Hills (c) Miri Hills (d) Naga Hills

218. Which is the chief river of Orissa?

(a) Brahmani (b) Subarnarekha (c) Mahanadi (d) Sileru

219. Which is the main oil centre in Assam?

(a) Dibrugarh (b) Digboi (c) Dum Dum (d) Tinsukia

220. Which is the chief town of the Chotanagpur plateau region?

(a) Khunti (b) Hazaribagh (c) Jamshedpur (d) Ranchi

221. Which was once a French possession in what is now West Bengal?

(a) Chandannagar (b) Haora (c) Chunchura (d) Kamarhati

222. On which river is Patna?

(a) Sapt Kosi (b) Son (c) Ganga (d) Damodar

223. Near which coastal pilgrim centre is Konarak?

(a) Chhatrapur (b) Puri (c) Ganjam (d) Baleshwar

224. Which is the chief town of Assam's northeastern tea country?

(a) Jorhat (b) Sibsagar (c) Dibrugarh (d) Tinsukia

225. Which city in Bihar is the centre of its mica mining activities?

(a) Munger (b) Kodarma (c) Jamshedpur (d) Dhanbad

226. Which is called the "Gateway to Western Sikkim"?

(a) Pemayangtse (b) Gangtok (c) Mangan (d) Lachen

227. Where is the Keibul Lamjao National Park?

(a) Assam, near Tezpur (b) Sikkim, near Gangtok (c) Manipur, near Loktak Lake (d) Arunachal Pradesh, near Tawang

228. Where exactly is the Visva Bharati University located?

(a) Kharagpur (b) Shantiniketan (c) Baliganj (d) Calcutta

229. What is the capital of Mizoram?

(a) Agartala (b) Imphal (c) Kohima (d) Aizawl

230. On which river is Diamond Harbour?

(a) Damodar (b) Ganga (c) Hughli (d) Bhagirathi

231. Which is the northernmost Buddhist pilgrim centre in Bihar?

(a) Bodh Gaya (b) Rajgir (c) Gaya (d) Vaishali

232. Where exactly is the Simplipal National Park?

(a) Northern Orissa (b) Southern West Bengal (c) Eastern Bihar (d) Near Chilika Lake

233. What was once a major Danish settlement in West Bengal?

(a) Chandannagar (b) Shrirampur (c) Chunchura (d) Barddhaman

234. What is called the "Mica Capital" of India?

(a) Dhanbad, Bihar (b) Raurkela, Orissa (c) Kodarma, Bihar (d) Durgapur, West Bengal

235. What is considered the most important commercial centre in Orissa?

(a) Bhubaneshwar (b) Berhampur (c) Paradwip (d) Cuttack

236. Which is West Bengal's best-known coastal
holiday resort?

(a) Digha (b) Garden Reach (c) Alipur
(d) Lakshmikantapur

237. Where is the longest bridge in India?

(a) Haora, West Bengal (b) Dehri-on-Son, Bihar
(c) Brahmaputra, Assam (d) Munger, Bihar

238. Where exactly is New Moore Island?

(a) In the Brahmaputra off Guwahati (b) Off
the Mahanadi Delta in Orissa (c) Off the mouth
of the Hughli (d) Off the Sundarbans, just inside
India's sea border with Bangladesh

239. Which major industrial centre straddles the
Bihar-West Bengal border?

(a) Burnpur (b) Asansol (c) Chittaranjan
(a) Durgapur

240. From where does the "toy train" to Darjeeling
start?

(a) Kalimpang (b) Siliguri (c) Jalpaiguri
(d) Kurseong

241. Which major town is near Orissa's biggest
damsite and reservoir?

(a) Sambalpur (b) Raurkela (c) Bolangir
(d) Sundargarh

242. With which countries does Assam have a
border?

(a) Nepal and Bhutan (b) Bhutan and Burma
(c) Bangladesh and Burma (d) Bhutan and
Bangladesh

243. On which river is the industrial town of
Durgapur?

(a) Hughli (b) Ganga (c) Damodar (d) Kasai

244. What is Gauhati now known as?

(a) Gowhati (b) Guwahati (c) Guhati (d) Gohati

245. Which is the highest peak in Orissa?

(a) Mahendragiri (b) Malayagiri (c) Megasini (d) Udayagiri

246. Which of the seven sisters remains a Union Territory?

(a) None (b) Arunachal Pradesh (c) Mizoram (d) Nagaland

247. Which major suburban city lies to the west of Calcutta, just across the Hugli?

(a) Baliganj (b) Taliganj (c) Kamarhati (d) Haora

248. Where is the Hindu pilgrim centre of Parasuram Kund?

(a) Assam (b) Arunachal Pradesh (c) Tripura (d) Meghalaya

249. Where does the Royal Bengal Tiger still survive?

(a) Simlipal, Orissa (b) Manas, Assam (c) The Sundarbans, West Bengal (d) Jaldapara, West Bengal

250. What is the capital of Nagaland?

(a) Kohima (b) Imphal (c) Aizawl (d) Silchar

V

WEST AND CENTRAL INDIA

Madhya Pradesh
Gujarat
Daman and Diu
Dadra and Nagar Haveli
Maharashtra
Goa

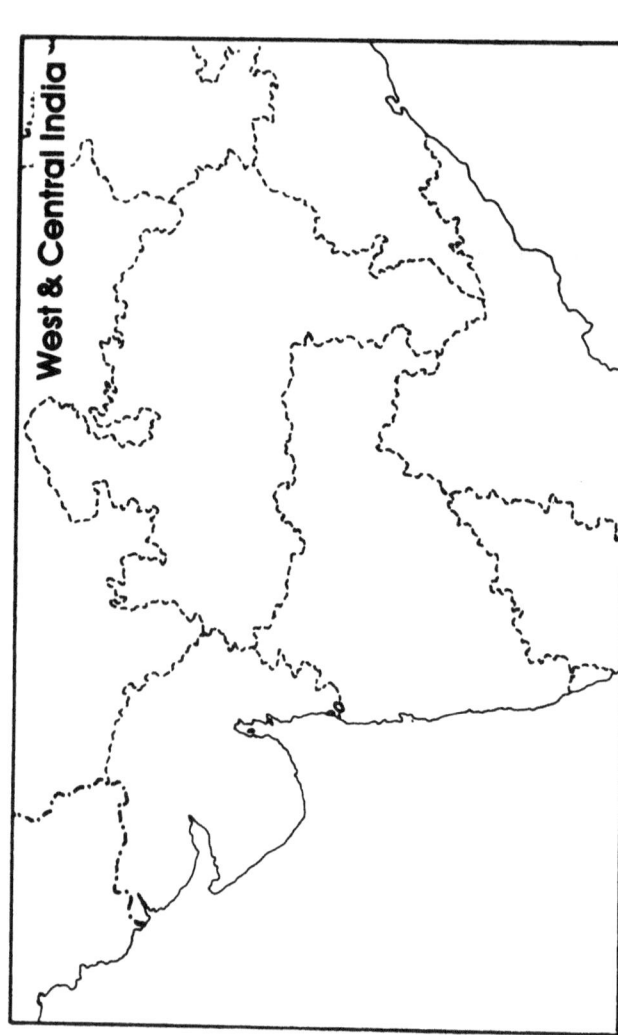

West & Central India

251. Where exactly is the Chhattisgarh plateau?

(a) Northern Maharashtra (b) Western Madhya Pradesh (c) Southern Gujarat (d) Eastern Madhya Pradesh

252. What is the language of the majority of people in the Union Territories of Daman and Diu?

(a) Gujarati (b) Marathi (c) Konkani (d) Portuguese

253. What are the two major mountain ranges in Madhya Pradesh?

(a) Kaimur and Maikala (b) Vindhyas and Satpuras (c) Mahadeo and Vindhyas (d) Bhanrer and Vindhyas

254. What are the two gulfs on either side of the Kathiawar peninsula?

(a) Palk and Mannar (b) Narmada and Indus (c) Kachchh and Khambat (d) Tapi and Indus

255. Which Union Territory is sandwiched between Gujarat and Maharashtra?

(a) Dadra and Nagar Haveli (b) Daman (c) Diu (d) Mahé

256. Near which important steel town are Durg and Raipur?

(a) Gwalior (b) Korba (c) Bhopal (d) Bhilai

257. What is the capital of Gujarat?

(a) Gandhinagar (b) Ahmadabad (c) Vadodara (d) Surat

258. Near which city is Ellora?

(a) Malegaon (b) Aurangabad (c) Nashik (d) Ahmadnagar

259. Where in Central India are diamonds mined?

(a) Palanpur, Gujarat (b) Shivpuri, Madhya Pradesh (c) Panna, Madhya Pradesh (d) Surat, Gujarat

260. Near which town is oil found in Gujarat?

(a) Ankleshwar (b) Vadodara (c) Bhavnagar (d) Surat

261. What is the Maharashtra coast called?

(a) The Surat Coast (b) The Khambat Coast (c) The Malabar Coast (d) The Konkan Coast

262. Which is considered the chief hill station of Gwalior?

(a) Morena (b) Shivpuri (c) Bhind (d) Datia

263. With what trade do you associate the town of Palanpur?

(a) Jewellery-making (b) Ceramicware (c) Diamond trading and polishing (d) Aluminiumware

264. What is Bassein now called?

(a) Vasai (b) Vasin (c) Bhasin (d) Basi

265. Which is the largest river flowing through Madhya Pradesh?

(a) Narmada (b) Mahanadi (c) Tapi (d) Son

266. What do Matheran, Lonavala, and Mahabaleshwar have in common?

(a) Fruit-growing centres in Maharashtra (b) Pilgrim centres in Maharashtra (c) Holiday resorts in coastal Maharashtra (d) Maharashtra hill stations in the Western Ghats

267. Which Gujarat district headquarters is the centre of the state's famed milk industry?

(a) Anand (b) Mahesana (c) Kalol (d) Patan

268. Which ancient Indian city, famed for its scholarship, is found in Madhya Pradesh?

(a) Ratlam (b) Indore (c) Ujjain (d) Vidisha

269. Which island off Bombay is a centre of cultural tourism?

(a) .Elephanta (b) Salsette (c) Colaba (d) Alibag

270. Near which river is Bhopal?

(a) Narmada (b) Betwa (c) Tapi (d) Parbati

271. What is another name for the Kathiawar Peninsula?

(a) Kachchh (b) Rajkot (c) Saurashtra (d) Jamnagar

272. Which major river forms part of the north-western boundary between Gujarat and Maharashtra?

(a) Girna (b) Sabarmati (c) Tapi (d) Narmada

273. Near which town are the Marble Rocks?

(a) Pachmarhi (b) Balaghat (c) Jabalpur (d) Sagar

274. What is Baroda now called?

(a) Vadodara (b) Barda (c) Varoda (d) Varda

275. Which river does the Bhima join?

(a) Godavari (b) Krishna (c) Dudhana (d) Sina

276. What is the salty marshland of northern Gujarat called?

(a) Kathiawar (b) Wild Ass Sanctuary (c) Southern Thar (d) The Rann of Kachchh

277. In which state or Union Territory are the northernmost reaches of the Western Ghats?

(a) Maharashtra (b) Madhya Fradesh (c) Gujarat (d) Daman

278. What is Ahmadabad's most important industry?

(a) Jewellery-making (b) Textiles (c) Chemicals (d) Engineering equipment

279. Near which town are the Girnar Hills?

(a) Somnath (b) Porbandar (c) Rajkot (d) Junagadh

280. Which other city in Maharashtra is considered a second administrative centre of the state?

(a) Nashik (b) Pune (c) Nagpur (d) Ahmadnagar

281. Where exactly is Bastar?

(a) In the narrow eastern stretch of Maharashtra (b) In the protruding southern finger of Madhya Pradesh (c) In the forests of Dadra and Nagar Haveli (d) In the westernmost area of Kachchh

282. Where is the last home of the Asian Lion?

(a) Gir Forest (b) Valavadar National Park (c) Bandhavgarh National Park (d) Tadoba National Park

283. Which two major east-flowing rivers have their beginnings in the Western Ghats?

(a) Narmada and Tapi (b) Tapi and Krishna (c) Narmada and Godavari (d) Godavari and Krishna

284. What do Mhow, Nimach, and Jabalpur have in common?

(a) Industrial towns (b) All are in Maharashtra (c) Cantonment towns (d) All are on the Narmada

285. Which are the two major pilgrim centres on the Kathiawar coast?

(a) Dwaraka and Somnath (b) Porbandar and Veraval (c) Dwaraka and Porbandar (d) Veraval and Somnath

286. Where exactly is the ancient town of Bagh?

(a) Near Gwalior (b) Near Indore (c) Near Bhopal (d) Near Ujjain

287. Which is the correct geographical name given to "Land's End" in Bombay?

(a) Elephanta (b) Salsette (c) Trombay (d) Colaba Point

288. Which area is famous for its white tigers?

(a) Bandhavgarh (b) Kanha (c) Rewa (d) Shivpuri

289. Where was the first British settlement established on the west coast of India?

(a) Bassein (b) Surat (c) Bombay (d) Diu

290. Where exactly is Baghelkhand?

(a) North-eastern M.P. (b) Southern M.P. (c) Northern M.P. (d) Western M.P.

291. Which is the new major harbour built in Maharashtra?

(a) Ratnagiri (b) Nav Sheva (c) Colaba (d) Salsette

292. What is the forested tribal area of Southern Gujarat known as?

(a) Khambat (b) Kathiawar (c) The Dangs (d) Gir Hills

293. Where exactly is the Melghat Tiger Reserve?

(a) North-eastern Maharashtra (b) Southern M.P. (c) Southern Gujarat (d) In the Balaghat Range

294. What is the capital of the largest Union Territory in Western India?

(a) Daman (b) Dadra (c) Diu (d) Silvassa

295. What separates Daman and Diu?

(a) Narmada River (b) The Gulf of Khambat
(c) Gir Hills (d) Tapi River

296. Where is the only nuclear power station in Western and Central India?

(a) Thane (b) Bandra (c) Borivili (d) Tarapur

297. Which river flows through Madhya Pradesh, Maharashtra, and Gujarat?

(a) Narmada (b) Godavari (c) Tapi (d) Mahi

298. Near which large town in Maharashtra is Gandhiji's famed Sevagram Ashram?

(a) Nagpur (b) Wardha (c) Amravati (d) Akola

299. Which place has been developed as an important port and Free Trade Zone in Gujarat?

(a) Kandla (b) Okha (c) Jamnagar (d) Porbandar

300. Where exactly is Salsette Island?

(a) Next to Diu (b) Off Surat (c) Near Bombay (d) By Alibag

VI

SOUTH ASIA
(but excluding India)

Afgnanistan
Pakistan
Nepal
Bhutan
Myanmar
Bangladesh
Sri Lanka
The Maldives
Indian Ocean

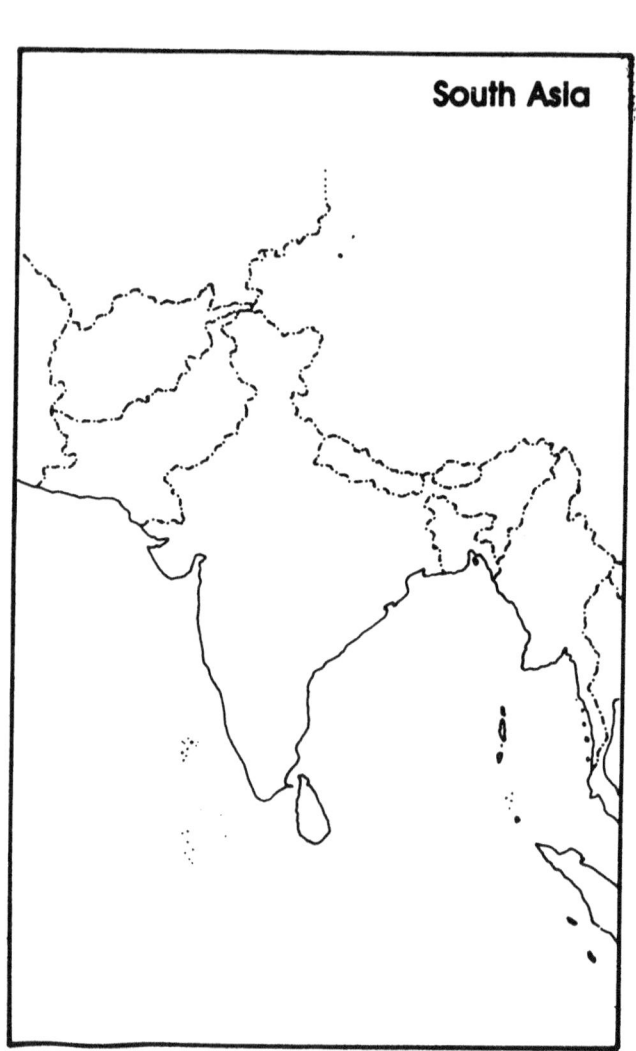

South Asia

301. Which town is Sri Lanka's major gem centre?

(a) Ratnapura (b) Galle (c) Kurunegala
(d) Gampola

302. Which is the most important river of Myanmar?

(a) Salween (b) Chindwin (c) Irrawaddy
(d) Sittang

303. Which is the mountain in Sri Lanka that is sacred to people of all faiths?

(a) Pidrutalagala (b) Nuwara Eliya (c) Hatton Hill (d) Adam's Peak

304. What is Lyallpur now called?

(a) Faisalabad (b) Lahore (c) Multan (d) Sargodha

305. What is the southernmost point in Sri Lanka?

(a) Galle (b) Dondra Head (c) Matara
(d) Hambantota

306. What deltaic jungle swampland does Bangladesh share with India?

(a) The Mouths of the Ganga (b) Sandwip (c) Chittagong Hill Tracts (d) The Sundarbans

307. Which South Indian city is airlinked to the Maldives?

(a) Tiruchchirappalli (b) Coimbatore
(c) Trivandrum (d) Calicut

308. Which is the legendary Pass which links Pakistan with Afghanistan?

(a) Khyber Pass (b) Bolan Pass (c) Chitral Pass
(d) Khojak Pass

309. Which is the best known place in the Chagos Archipelago?

(a) Crozet (b) Diego Garcia (c) Gan (d) New Amsterdam

310. Near which capital city is Taxila?

(a) Kabul (b) Kathmandu (c) Islamabad (d) Thimphu

311. Which South Asian country is famous for its ruby mines?

(a) Myanmar (b) Sri Lanka (c) Pakistan (d) Bhutan

312. In which country is jute the principal foreign exchange earner?

(a) Pakistan (b) Sri Lanka (c) Bangladesh (d) Myanmar

313. What is the highest peak in Nepal?

(a) Dhaulagiri (b) Kanchenjunga (c) Annapurna (d) Mount Everest

314. To which country did the Maldives once pay annual tribute?

(a) Sri Lanka (b) India (c) Pakistan (d) Afghanistan

315. With which country/countries in this region does Pakistan have borders?

(a) Only Afghanistan (b) Afghanistan and Nepal (c) Afghanistan and India (d) Only India

316. Gan was once an important British air base. In which country is it?

(a) Sri Lanka (b) The Maldives (c) Pakistan (d) Bangladesh

317. Which countries does the Karakoram Highway join?

(a) Pakistan and China via India (b) Pakistan and Nepal (c) India and China (d) Pakistan and India

318. Which is Sri Lanka's largest natural harbour?

(a) Colombo (b) Galle (c) Trincomalee
(d) Kankesanturai

319. Which major cities of the Indian and Pakistani Punjab are directly linked by train?

(a) Amritsar and Sialkot (b) Lahore and Jalandhar (c) Ferozpur and Lahore (d) Amritsar and Lahore

320. In which country would you expect to find a large Gurkha population?

(a) Nepal (b) Bhutan (c) Myanmar
(d) Bangladesh

321. What is Piduratalagala's special feature?

(a) It is a sacred peak in Sri Lanka (b) It is the highest peak in Sri Lanka (c) It is a mining town in Sri Lanka (d) It is a wildlife sanctuary in Sri Lanka

322. Which country does a large export trade in Karakul skins?

(a) Pakistan (b) Bhutan (c) Afghanistan
(d) Nepal

323. What is significant about Landi Kotal?

(a) It is the Pakistan railway terminus before the Khyber Pass (b) It is a big fort in Pakistan (c) It is a new industrial city in Pakistan (d) It is a town of archaeological significance in Pakistan

324. Which is the capital of Bhutan?

(a) Patan (b) Thimphu (c) Namche Bazar
(d) Phuntsholing

325. On which river is the Tarbela Dam?

(a) Satluj (b) Jhelum (c) Indus (d) Ravi

326. What is the southernmost group of islands in the Maldives?

(a) Mulaku (b) Nilandu (c) Huvadu (d) Addu Atoll/Sennu

327. Which is the hill station of Pakistan's capital?

(a) Rawalpindi (b) Murree (c) Peshawar (d) Abbottabad

328. Where is Lumbini and what is it famous for?

(a) In Bhutan, where there is a famous Bo tree (b) In Myanmar, where rubies are mined (c) In Bangladesh, where the Ganga and Brahmaputra join (d) In Nepal, where Lord Buddha was born

329. In which country in this region would you find island groups called atolls?

(a) Maldives (b) Bangladesh (c) Pakistan (d) Myanmar

330. For what timber is Myanmar famous?

(a) Rosewood (b) Satinwood (c) Teak (d) Jak

331. Which is the southernmost major tributary of the Indus river?

(a) Jhelum (b) Beas (c) Ravi (d) Satluj

332. What is Rangoon now known as?

(a) Yangon (b) Angoon (c) Rangon (d) Yangoon

333. From which major town in western Afghanistan does a highway run into the Soviet Union?

(a) Balkh (b) Herat (c) Kabul (d) Kandahar

334. Which is Bangladesh's major port?

(a) Cox's Bazar (b) Barguna (c) Chittagong (d) Sandwip

335. Which is the largest city in Pakistan?

(a) Karachi ·(b) Islamabad (c) Peshawar
(d) Rawalpindi

336. Which is the "Hill Capital" of Sri Lanka?

(a) Nuwara Eliya (b) Kandy (c) Badulla
(d) Hatton

337. Which two border towns face each other on
the main road from India to Kathmandu?

(a) Bahraich and Nepalganj (b) Lakhimpur and
Kumbher (c) Jogbani and Biratnagar (d) Bir-
ganj and Raxaul

338. Which major river in Myanmar forms part of
the boundary with Thailand?

(a) Irrawaddy (b) Chindwin (c) Salween
(d) Sittang

339. Which is the chief town of Sri Lanka's Northern
Province?

(a) Jaffna (b) Mannar (c) Vavuniya (d) Trincomalee

340. Which major archaeological site associated with
early civilisation is near Larkana?

(a) Mohen-Jo-Daro (b) Sukkur (c) Dadu
(d) Kashmor

341. Which are the two major coastal towns on
either side of the Gulf of Martaban?

(a) Akyab and Pegu (b) Bangkok and Yangon
(c) Medan and Pinang (d) Yangon and Moulmein

342. Where is the Ganga called the Padma?

(a) In Bangladesh (b) In Nepal (c) In Bhutan
(d) In Myanmar

343. Where is Lashio and why is it significant?

(a) An oil town in Myanmar (b) A ruby mining
centre in Myanmar (c) A rail terminus in

Myanmar from which a World War II highway leads to China (d) A major port on the Irrawaddy

344. Which major provincial capital in western Pakistan is entered through the Bolan Pass?

(a) Peshawar (b) Quetta (c) Karachi (d) Surab

345. Which major port of Myanmar is on the Bay of Bengal?

(a) Basseien (b) Akyab (c) Yangon (d) Moulmein

346. What is Namche Bazar famous for?

(a) The view of the Himalaya (b) A Gurkha recruiting station (c) Starting point for those climbing Everest (d) The biggest suburb of Kathmandu

347. What is the major export of the Maldives?

(a) Fish (b) Copra (c) Coral (d) Lime

348. Which Indian state or states separate Nepal and Bhutan?

(a) Bihar and Sikkim (b) Bihar and West Bengal (c) West Bengal and Meghalaya (d) Sikkim and West Bengal

349. What does the Brahmaputra flow into Bangladesh as?

(a) Jamuna (b) Madhumati (c) Padma (d) Meghna

350. Which major town in Sind has the same name as a major city in the Deccan?

(a) Khairpur (b) Hyderabad (c) Nawabshah (d) Uthal

351. How many islands in the Maldives are officially stated to be inhabited?

(a) 185 (b) 403 (c) 116 (d) 204

352. Which river does the Ganga join in Bangladesh and flow out to the sea as?

    (a) Meghna (b) Padma (c) Jamuna (d) Madhumati

353. With which country does Nepal share its northern border?

    (a) USSR (b) Bhutan (c) China (d) India

354. What is the name of the "pass" that links the northern peninsula with the rest of Sri Lanka?

    (a) Point Pedro Causeway (b) Elephant Pass (c) Mullaitivu Causeway (d) Mannar Bridge

355. Where exactly is the Hindu Kush?

    (a) In Western Afghanistan (b) In Northern Pakistan (c) On either side of the Khyber Pass (d) Just north of Kabul

356. On what island is Male's airport?

    (a) Hulule (b) Gan (c) Felidu (d) Nilandu

357. What is the name of the major reservoir developed by impounding the water of the Gal Oya in eastern Sri Lanka?

    (a) Bandaranaike Sea (b) Senanayake Samudra (c) Jayawardenapura (d) Sirima Wewa

358. Which is the northernmost of the five major tributaries of the Indus?

    (a) Ravi (b) Beas (c) Jhelum (d) Chenab

359. From which town in Afghanistan does the northern highway to Teheran run?

    (a) Kabul (b) Kushka (c) Farah (d) Herat

360. What is the name of the southernmost mountain range in Pakistan?

(a) Makran (b) Sulaiman (c) Hindu Kush (d) Salt Range

361. What is the westernmost coastal region of Myanmar called?

(a) Akyab (b) Arakan (c) Chittagong Hill Tracts (d) Chin Hills

362. To which famous landmark is Peshawar the nearest provincial capital?

(a) Bolan Pass (b) Landi Kotal Fort (c) Khyber Pass (d) Attock Fort

363. What is the tribal region of Bangladesh called?

(a) Sundarbans (b) Meghna Delta (c) Kutubdia Island (d) Chittagong Hill Tracts

364. What is Sagarmata better known as?

(a) Everest (b) Annapurna (c) Kanchenjunga (d) Nanda Devi

365. How many islands are believed to be there in the Maldives?

(a) About 250 (b) About 4000 (c) About 2000 (d) About 600

366. On what river is the Sukkur Barrage?

(a) Beas (b) Indus (c) Ravi (d) Satluj

367. With which Indian states does Nepal have a boundary?

(a) Himachal Pradesh, Uttar Pradesh, Bihar (b) Jammu and Kashmir, Himachal Pradesh, and Uttar Pradesh (c) Assam, West Bengal and Sikkim (d) Uttar Pradesh, Bihar, West Bengal and Sikkim

368. What is sometimes called the Dragon Kingdom?

(a) Bhutan (b) Nepal (c) Sikkim (d) Nagaland

369. What is Patan in Nepal also known as?

(a) Kathmandu (b) Lalitpur (c) Gorkha (d) Bhadgaon

370. Which water body separates the southernmost Myanmar territory and India?

(a) Gulf of Martaban (b) The Bay of Bengal (c) The Andaman Sea (d) The Coco Channel

371. Which is the biggest of the landlocked countries of this region?

(a) Pakistan (b) Afghanistan (c) Bhutan (d) Nepal

372. What specifically do Annapurna, Makalu and Dhaulagiri have in common?

(a) All are Himalayan peaks (b) All are over 8,500 m (c) All are mountain peaks in Nepal (d) All are on Nepal's borders

373. In which Bangladesh province are most of the mouths of the Ganga?

(a) Khulna (b) Dacca (c) Rajshahi (d) Chittagong

374. Which is the largest province in Pakistan?

(a) Punjab (b) Baluchistan (c) Sind (d) NWFP

375. What do Anuradhapura, Sigiriya, and Polonnaruwa have in common?

(a) All major cities in Sri Lanka (b) All Sri Lankan holiday resorts (c) All forest-girt towns in Sri Lanka (d) All ancient capitals of Sri Lanka

376. Which place dating to an ancient civilisation is near Sahiwal?

(a) Mohen-jo-Daro (b) Harappa (c) Uthal (d) Taxila

377. Which is the capital of Sri Lanka's Eastern Province?

(a) Batticaloa (b) Trincomalee (c) Kalmunai
(d) Pottuvil

378. What do the initials NWFP stand for?

(a) North-West Federal Province (b) New
Western Federal Province (c) North-West Frontier Province (d) North-West Fiscal Province

379. Which is the capital of Afghanistan?

(a) Kandahar (b) Herat (c) Kunduz (d) Kabul

380. Which mountain range is to be found in the south-western part of Nepal?

(a) Himalaya (b) Kumaun Hills (c) The Shiwaliks (d) The Tarai

381. In which Pakistan city is the sports goods industry a major one?

(a) Sialkot (b) Karachi (c) Multan (d) Lahore

382. Which is the centre of the mineral product industry in Myanmar?

(a) Mandalay (b) Moulmein (c) Yenangyang (d) Myitkyina

383. Name the three central rivers of the Pakistan Punjab in the correct order from north to south:

(a) Satluj, Ravi, Beas (b) Jhelum, Chenab, Ravi (c) Beas, Jhelum, Satluj (d) Chenab, Beas and Ravi

384. Which southern harbour was once Sri Lanka's most important?

(a) Hambantota (b) Galle (c) Matara (d) Dondra

385. In exactly which part of which country in this region would you find the Doab?

(a) Southern Nepal (b) Western Afghanistan (c) Pakistan Punjab (d) Meghna Delta

386. In which area is most of Sri Lanka's tea grown?

(a) In the central highlands (b) In the western plains (c) In the Vanni (d) In the Mahaweli valley

387. What is the "correct" name of the Sukkur Barrage?

(a) Jinnah Barrage (b) Lloyd Barrage (c) The Indus Barrage (d) The Lawrence Barrage

388. In which country would you expect to find the Drukpas?

(a) Nepal (b) Myanmar (c) Maldives (d) Bhutan

389. In which country in the region is graphite an important mineral extraction?

(a) Afghanistan (b) Pakistan (c) Sri Lanka (d) Bhutan

390. Where would you expect to find the Sultan of Swat, if he existed?

(a) In the northern reaches of the NWFP in Pakistan (b) In western Afghanistan (c) In Pakistan's Baluchistan Province (d) In northern Afghanistan

391. Once India was linked with Sri Lanka by a ferry service. What was the port that served it in Sri Lanka?

(a) Mannar (b) Talaimannar (c) Kankesanturai (d) Point Pedro

392. Which major city is considered the "cantonment" of Pakistan's capital?

(a) Attock (b) Abbotabad (c) Rawalpindi (d) Peshawar

393. Which Indian state do Bhutan and Nepal almost completely sandwich?

(a) Sikkim (b) West Bengal (c) Assam
(d) Meghalaya

394. Which new port in Pakistan is being developed as a major labour and industrial centre?

(a) Gwadar, west of Karachi (b) Port Qasim, east of Karachi (c) Ormera, west of Karachi (d) Keti Bander, east of Karachi

395. Which is the biggest city in central Myanmar?

(a) Prome (b) Pegu (c) Myitkyina (d) Mandalay

396. In which Pakistan province is Pushtu the major language?

(a) Sind (b) Baluchistan (c) NWFP (d) Punjab

397. Where would you find the Shan, Kachin, Chin, and Karen states?

(a) Afghanistan (b) Bhutan (c) Nepal
(d) Myanmar

398. What is the geographical name for the Pakistan coast?

(a) Makran Coast (b) Karachi Coast
(c) Gwadar Coast (d) Indus Coast

399. Near which important city in Bangladesh is tea the major crop?

(a) Dhaka (b) Sylhet (c) Chittagong (d) Cox's Bazar

400. Which is the first immigration post in Pakistan across the border from Atari?

(a) Lahore (b) Wagah (c) Narowal (d) Kasur

VII

THE REST OF ASIA

Asia, excluding
the whole of
South Asia
and including
Asian Russia

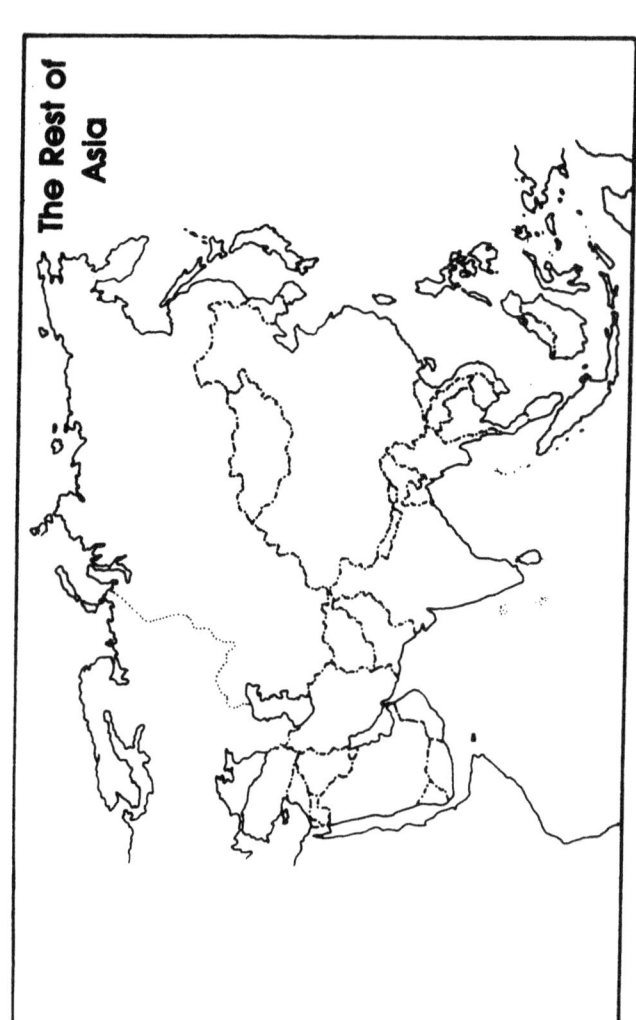

The Rest of Asia

401. Which Thai town is called by a variation of the name of an ancient Indian city?

(a) Buriram (b) Ayutthaya (c) Uttaradit (d) Chaiyaphum

402. Which is Beijing's port?

(a) Tianjin (b) Luda (c) Qingdao (d) Yantai

403. On which island is the capital of Indonesia?

(a) Sumatra (b) Bali (c) Sulawesi (d) Java

404. Which is Yemen's most important port?

(a) Al Mukalla (b) Al Luhayyah (c) Aden (d) Al Hudaydah

405. Shikoku, Hokkaido and Honshu. What is the fourth name in this set?

(a) Kyushu (b) Ryukyu (c) Sakhalin (d) Kuril

406. Which is the mountain chain just south of the Caspian Sea?

(a) Koppet Dagh (b) Elburz (c) Araks (d) Caucasus

407. With which country does Laos have a common eastern border?

(a) Thailand (b) Cambodia (c) China (d) Vietnam

408. The West Bank is claimed by Israel as its own. What is this area west of?

(a) River Jordan (b) Jordan (c) Dead Sea (d) Amman

409. On which island is George Town?

(a) Singapore (b) Penang (c) Langkawi (d) Phuket

410. Which countries does the Amur separate?

(a) China and Russia (b) China and Mongolia (c) China and Myanmar (d) China and Vietnam

411. What is another name for Cambodia?

(a) Indo-China (b) Vietnam (c) Camboge (d) Kampuchea

412. Which two countries are divided by the 38th Parallel?

(a) Vietnam and Cambodia (b) U S S R and China (c) North and South Korea (d) China and North Korea

413. Which is Tokyo's port?

(a) Yokohama (b) Osaka (c) Kobe (d) Nagoya

414. What is Siam now known as?

(a) Cambodia (b) Thailand (c) Vietnam (d) Laos

415. Most of which country is occupied by the Anatolian plateau?

(a) Iran (b) Syria (c) Turkey (d) Iraq

416. By what name is the southern China city of Guangzhou more familiarly known to us?

(a) Changsha (b) Chungking (c) Quanzhou (d) Canton

417. Which is the biggest oil-refining centre in Iran?

(a) Abadan (b) Bushehr (c) Shiraz (d) Dezful

418. What are Dairen and Port Arthur known as today?

(a) Lushun (b) Luda (c) Yantai (d) Dandong

419. Into which city is the town of Jaffa now incorporated?

(a) Haifa (b) Tiberia (c) Tel Aviv (d) Acre

420. What is the Brahmaputra called in Tibet?

(a) Tsang-po (b) Salween (c) Yangtse (d) Mekong

421. This Gulf nation is a peninsula. What is its name?

(a) Bahrain (b) Qatar (c) Oman (d) Kuwait

422. With which water body do you associate the world's best caviar?

(a) The Caspian Sea (b) The Volga river (c) The Aral Sea (d) The Ob river

423. What separates Sumatera and Malaysia?

(a) The Mergui Archipelago (b) The Gulf of Siam (c) The Java Sea (d) The Malacca Straits

424. Which is the town which gives Israel access to the Red Sea?

(a) Aqaba (b) Gaza (c) Eilat (d) Negev

425. Which countries does the Strait of Hormuz separate?

(a) UAE and Oman (b) Oman and Iran (c) Bahrain and Qatar (d) Iran and UAE

426. Which is the southernmost of the major islands in the Philippines?

(a) Mindanao (b) Luzon (c) Leyte (d) Negros

427. Of which important city is Jeddah the port?

(a) Riyadh (b) Mecca (c) Medina (d) Dhahran

428. In which country are the famous Angkor Wat ruins?

(a) Thailand (b) Vietnam (c) Cambodia (d) Laos

429. In which Soviet republic is the ancient town of Samarkand?

(a) Uzbek Republic (b) Kazakh Republic (c) Turkmen Republic (d) Tadzhik Republic

430. Which country in this region is the world's largest producer of tin concentrates?

(a) China (b) Malaysia (c) Thailand (d) Indonesia

431. Which is the city with the largest population in China?

(a) Beijing (b) Nanjing (c) Shanghai (d) Wuhan

432. What do many people living in our part of the world incorrectly call the Middle East?

(a) The Arabian Peninsula (b) The Gulf countries (c) The Anatolian region (d) West Asia

433. Which country considers the Yalu as its most navigable river?

(a) North Korea (b) Vietnam (c) Mongolia (d) South Korea

434. Which is the city with the largest population in the Asian USSR?

(a) Irkutsk (b) Vladivostok (c) Tashkent (d) Novosibirsk

435. Which is the capital of Cambodia?

(a) Vientiane (b) Phnom Penh (c) Hanoi (d) Pyongyang

436. What is the chief agricultural activity of Mongolia?

(a) Stock-raising (b) Wheat-growing (c) Horticulture (d) Sheep-farming

437. In which country is the Negev Desert?

(a) Syria (b) Jordan (c) Saudi Arabia (d) Israel

438. With the export of which cash crop was the port of Mokha long associated?

(a) Coffee (b) Dates (c) Lemons (d) Raisins

439. The UAE separates two parts of a country. Which country?

(a) Saudi Arabia (b) Qatar (c) Oman (d) Yemen

440. Which "Gulf country" is an island?

(a) Kuwait (b) Qatar (c) Bahrain (d) UAE

441. Which is the largest republic of Russia entirely in Asia?

(a) Kazakh Republic (b) Uzbek Republic (c) Kirghiz Republic (d) Turkmen Republic

442. Which Mediterranean island is considered an independent Asian country?

(a) Malta (b) Cyprus (c) Crete (d) Rhodes

443. Most of the Russian republics in Asia comprise what well known geographic area?

(a) Steppes (b) Taiga (c) Siberia (d) Ob valley

444. What capital city would you find in the delta of the Red River?

(a) Pyongyang (b) Seoul (c) Vientiane (d) Hanoi

445. Where is the Dead Sea?

(a) Jordan-Israel (b) Jordan-Syria (c) Israel-Lebanon (d) Syria-Lebanon

446. Of which country is Sarawak a part?

(a) Indonesia (b) Malaysia (c) Singapore (d) The Philippines

447. What is Mesopotamia now called?

(a) Iran (b) Saudi Arabia (c) Iraq (d) Lebanon

448. What was the old capital of the Philippines?

(a) Baguio (b) Davao (c) Cebu (d) Quezon City

449. The Euphrates is one of Iraq's major rivers. What is the other?

(a) Tigris (b) Jordan (c) Karun (d) Shatt-al-Arab

450. Of which country is Irian Jaya a part?

(a) The Philippines (b) Vietnam (c) Malaysia (d) Indonesia

451. Which Chinese province has some of the largest· reserves of coal and iron ore in the world?

(a) Hunan (b) Liaoning (c) Shanxi (d) Shandong

452. What do the Makasar Straits separate?

(a) Kalimantan and Sulawesi (b) Peninsular Malaysia and Sarawak (c) Sumatera and Kalimantan (d) The Greater Sundas and Lesser Sundas

453. To which Iranian city does the railway from Pakistan extend?

(a) Mashad (b) Zahedan (c) Kerman (d) Yazd

454. What is the name of the sea that separates European and Asian Turkey?

(a) Black Sea (b) Mediterranean Sea (c) Dead Sea (d) Sea of Marmara

455. What is Saigon now known as?

(a) Ho Chi Minh City (b) Haiphong (c) Da Nang (d) An Nhon

456. In which republic is Tashkent?

(a) Kirghiz Republic (b) Tadzhik Republic (c) Uzbek Republic (d) Turkmen Republic

457. Which part of Egypt is in Asia?

(a) Gaza (b) Sinai Peninsula (c) Suez (d) The Bitter Lakes

458. Of the three major rivers of Asian Russia, which is the centremost?

(a) Ob (b) Lena (c) Yenisey (d) Kolyma

459. Of which country is Beirut the capital?

(a) Syria (b) Lebanon (c) Jordan (d) Qatar

460. Which countries once formed the territory called French Indo-China?

(a) Laos, Cambodia and Vietnam (b) The two Koreas (c) Thailand and Cambodia (d) Vietnam, Thailand, and Laos

461. What are the two straits that ships bound for the Black Sea from the Mediterranean have to pass through?

(a) Marmara and Aegean (b) Istanbul and Aegean (c) Istanbul and Rhodes (d) The Dardenelles and the Bosporous

462. What do the Ural mountains separate?

(a) European and Asian Russia (b) The Pripet Marshes and the Steppes (c) Ukraine Republic and Russian Republic (d) Kazakh Republic and Russian Republic

463. What is significant about Vladivostock?

(a) Siberia's biggest city (b) A major fishing centre (c) Russia's major eastern port (d) The only port in Siberia

464. Of which country are phosphates its most important resource?

(a) Syria (b) Jordan (c) Saudi Arabia (d) Iraq

465. Near which large lake in the mountains of Siberia is Irkutsk?

(a) Aral Sea (b) Lake Balkash (c) Lake Zaysan (d) Lake Baikal

466. Which is the capital of Tibet?

(a) Lhasa (b) Gyangtse (c) Shigatse
(d) Chengtu

467. The Isthmus of Kra is a narrow neck of land in which one country ends and another extends. What are the two countries?

(a) Malaysia and Thailand (b) Myanmar and Thailand (c) Myanmar and Malaysia (d) Malaysia and Singapore

468. Which country is the largest producer of wolfram (tungsten ore) in the world?

(a) China (b) Malaysia (c) Indonesia (d) North Korea

469. Of which country is Ulan Bator the capital?

(a) Indonesia (b) Mongolia (c) North Korea (d) Laos

470. Where exactly is Manchuria?

(a) North-western China (b) Eastern Mongolia (c) North-eastern corner of China (d) Southern Siberia

471. Which independent island country does China claim as one of its provinces?

(a) Hong Kong (b) Taiwan (c) The Philippines (d) Japan

472. Which countries border the Sea of Galilee?

(a) Lebanon, Syria, and Israel (b) Lebanon, Jordan, and Israel (c) Israel, Jordan, and Egypt (d) Israel, Jordan, and Syria (before Israeli occupation of its territory here)

473. What is Indonesian Borneo called?

(a) Kalimantan (b) Sulawesi (c) Maluku (d) Irian Jaya

474. What is Mongolia's great desert called?

(a) Great Mongolian Desert (b) Gobi Desert (c) China Desert (d) Siberian Desert

475. Three Japanese cities are so large, they have almost begun to merge with each other. Which are they?

(a) Nagoya, Kyoto, and Kobe (b) Tokyo, Yokohama, and Kobe (c) Kobe, Osaka, and Kyoto (d) Kobe, Osaka, and Nara

476. Which famous island in the Arabian Sea is a part of Yemen?

(a) Socotra (b) Aden (c) Abdal Kuri (d) Kuria Muria

477. Near which northern town are the main oilfields of Iraq?

(a) Kirkuk (b) Mosul (c) Samarra (d) Erbil

478. In which country is Phuket, a well-known tourist resort?

(a) Malaysia (b) Indonesia (c) Cambodia (d) Thailand

479. Which is the capital of Saudi Arabia?

(a) Riyadh (b) Mecca (c) Medina (d) Dhahran

480. Which Malaysian town is the crossing point to Singapore?

(a) Melaka (b) Johor Bahru (c) Kelang (d) Port Dickson

481. What is Formosa now known as?

(a) Taipei (b) Tainan (c) Taiwan (d) Taichung

482. From which Iraqi city does the oil pipeline run to Mediterranean ports?

(a) Basra (b) Baghdad (c) Mosul (d) Kirkuk

483. Which large Chinese, or Chinese-claimed, island lies in the mouth of the Gulf of Tongking?

(a) Hainan (b) Paracel (c) Cheju (d) Hong Kong

484. Which is the capital of North Korea?

(a) Chongjin (b) Pyongyang (c) Pusan (d) Wonsan

485. The Kirghiz steppes are, for the most part, in which Russian republic?

(a) Kirghiz Republic (b) Uzbek Republic (c) Kazakh Republic (d) Tadzhik Republic

486. What is China's westernmost province or autonomous region?

(a) Xinjiang-Uygur (b) Tibet Autonomous Region (c) Qinghai (d) Gansu

487. Of which territory is Kowloon the land portion?

(a) Paracel Islands (b) Hong Kong (c) Hainan (d) Shantung Peninsula

488. Where would you find the Roof of the World?

(a) Tsang-po Valley (b) Tibetan Himalaya (c) Kunlun Mountains (d) Pamir Plateau in Tibet

489. Istanbul is better known than its capital. What is the country and its capital?

(a) Lebanon, Beirut (b) Syria, Damascus (c) Turkey, Ankara (d) Suadi Arabia, Riyadh

490. On which island is Nagasaki?

(a) Kyushu (b) Honshu (c) Okinawa (d) Shikoku

491. With which countries does Iraq have a common border on its south?

(a) Jordan and Saudi Arabia (b) Saudi Arabia and Kuwait (c) Kuwait and Iran (d) Syria and Jordan

492. Which major island, the subject of dispute between the USSR and Japan, lies in the Sea of Okhotsk?

(a) Sakhalin (b) Kuril (c) Hokkaido (d) Sado

493. What was Port Kelang once known as?

(a) Port Dickson (b) George Town (c) Port Butterworth (d) Port Swettenham

494. Which inland sea is in the Asian landmass of Russia?

(a) Aral Sea (b) Caspian Sea (c) Dead Sea (d) Balkhash Sea

495. Of which island chain is Okinawa a part?

(a) Kuril Islands (b) Sakhalin Islands (c) Ryukyu Islands (d) Bonin Islands

496. What do these three territories have in common: Umm al Qawain, Ras al Khaimah and Fujairah?

(a) Islands in the Gulf (b) Towns in Saudi Arabia (c) All British protectorates in West Asia (d) Three of the United Arab Emirates

497. Which is the northernmost of the major Indonesian islands?

(a) Sumatera (b) Java (c) Kalimantan (d) Sulawesi

498. What is the name of the Portuguese colony in China?

(a) Hong Kong (b) Macao (c) Hainan (d) Kowloon

499. On what island is the capital of the Philippines?

(a) Negros (b) Mindanao (c) Luzon (d) Panay

500. What is the familiar name of China's longest river?

(a) Red River (b) Yangtze-Kiang (c) Yellow River (d) Amur River

VIII

AFRICA

Including
the islands
off both
its coasts

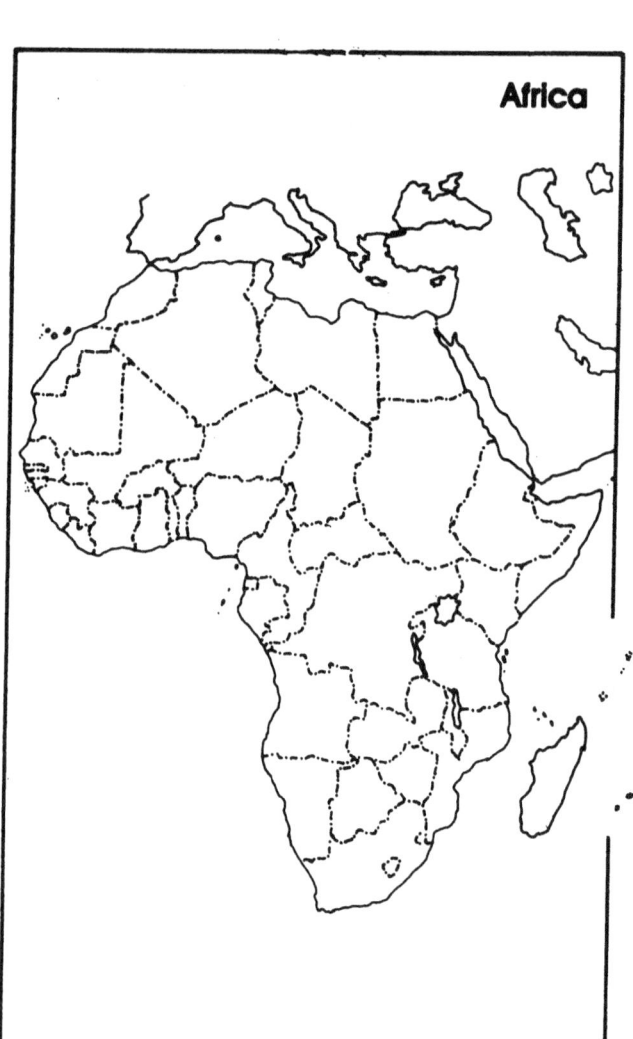

Africa

501. Of which country is Freetown the capital?

(a) Liberia (b) Ghana (c) Nigeria (d) Sierra Leone

502. What is Leopoldville now called?

(a) Kinshasa (b) Kisangani (c) Kananga (d) Kamina

503. In the middle of which country is Timbuktu (Tomboctou)?

(a) Mauritania (b) Mali (c) Algeria (d) Niger

504. Which nation of islands is to the west of the central African coast?

(a) Cabinda (b) Equatorial Guinea (c) Sao Tomé E Principé (d) Pagalu

505. Where is Serengeti National Park?

(a) Tanzania (b) Kenya (c) Uganda (d) Malawi

506. With which river do you associate the colours Blue and White?

(a) Zaire (b) Nile (c) Zambezi (d) Orange

507. Which was the occupying power in Western Sahara and which is the present power?

(a) Spain and Morocco (b) France and Mauritania (c) France and Algeria (d) Germany and Morocco

508. Which countries have parts of their boundaries in Lake Victoria?

(a) Rwanda and Burundi (b) Ethiopia, Uganda, and Rwanda (c) Tanzania and Burundi (d) Uganda, Kenya, and Tanzania

509. The coast of which country is called the Gold Coast?

(a) Togo (b) Ghana (c) Benin (d) Nigeria

510. Which is the main port of Kenya?

(a) Malindi (b) Kisumu (c) Mombasa (d) Kalindini

511. This country's mainland is bigger than its island half. Yet its capital is on the island. What is this country and what is its capital?

(a) Equatorial Guinea; Malabo (b) Sao Tomé E Principé; Sao Tomé, (c) Angola; Cabinda (d) Comoro; Moroni

512. What was Malawi once called?

(a) Gold Coast (b) Nyasaland (c) Upper Volta (d) Dahomey

513. In which country would you find the Ahaggar (Hoggar) mountains?

(a) Algeria (b) Morocco (c) Tunisia (d) Libya

514. How did Tanzania get its name?

(a) The Swahili version of Tanganyika (b) The ancient name of the region (c) From a nearby lake (d) When Tanganyika and Zanzibar became one

515. Which is the largest lake in West Africa?

(a) Lake Kainji (b) Lake Faguibire (c) Lake Volta (d) Lake Chad

516. Which group of islands is a nation just north-east of Madagascar?

(a) The Seychelles (b) Comoro (c) Mauritius (d) Reunion

517. Which was the country freed slaves from the USA founded in Africa?

(a) Ivory Coast (b) Liberia (c) Sierra Leone (d) Gambia

518. One island in the Comoros Group has a different political status. Which one?

(a) Reunion (b) Moheli (c) Grand Comore (d) Mayotte

519. What is South-west Africa now called?

(a) Botswana (b) Angola (c) Namibia (d) Lesotho

520. With which West African country is Pagalu linked?

(a) Equatorial Guinea (b) Gabon (c) Congo (d) Cameroon

521. In which country would you expect to find the Copper Belt?

(a) Zimbabwe (b) Zambia (c) Zaire (d) Mozambique

522. Two neighbouring African countries get their names from a river they share. What is the name of the river?

(a) Zaire (b) Orange (c) Niger (d) Zambezi

523. Which city lies in the shadow of Table Mountain?

(a) Durban (b) Walvis Bay (c) Port Elizabeth (d) Cape Town

524. To whom do the Azores and the Canary Islands belong?

(a) Azores (Portugal); Canaries (Spain)
(b) Azores (France); Canaries (U.K.)
(c) Azores (Spain); Canaries (France)
(d) Azores (Mauritania); Canaries (Morocco)

525. Which is the capital of Zaire?

(a) Kisangani (b) Kinshasa (c) Lubumbashi (d) Matadi

526. Of which country is the Ogaden a region?

(a) Sudan (b) Egypt (c) Ethiopia (d) Somalia

527. Which are the two small countries sandwiched by the borders of Uganda and Tanzania?

(a) Swaziland and Lesotho (b) Malawi and Burundi (c) Malawi and Rwanda (d) Rwanda and Burundi

528. By which river delta is Port Harcourt located?

(a) Niger (b) Zambezi (c) Vaal (d) Zaire

529. What is the narrow feature that separates Africa from Asia?

(a) Sinai (b) The Suez Canal (c) The Horn (d) The Red Sea

530. Which country is completely landlocked by South Africa?

(a) Swaziland (b) Botswana (c) Lesotho (d) Zimbabwe

531. Between which countries is Togo sandwiched?

(a) Benin and Nigeria (b) Ghana and Ivory Coast (c) Ivory Coast and Burkina Faso (d) Ghana and Benin

532. With which of its southern neighbours does Libya have the longest boundary?

(a) Chad (b) Niger (c) Sudan (d) Algeria

533. What was the name under which two West African countries federated for a while a few years ago?

(a) Tanzania (b) Senegambia (c) Rhodesia (d) Senegal

534. What are Transkei, Venda, and Ciskei?

(a) The ancient names of Pretoria, Cape Town, and Durban (b) The capitals of Botswana, Lesotho, and Swaziland (c) Rivers in South

Africa (d) South African tribal homelands with a degree of self-government

535. Which is the capital of Madagascar?

(a) Antananarivo (b) Tamatave (c) Majunga (d) Tulear

536. What is Nigeria's main export?

(a) Iron ore (b) Maize (c) Oil (d) Gold

537. Which island nation, geographically considered part of Africa, has an Indian population in the majority?

(a) Reunion (b) Mauritius (c) Comoro (d) Madagascar

538. Where in Africa would you find the Mahgreb?

(a) Moorish Africa — Morocco, Algeria, and Tunisia (b) Libya and Egypt (c) Along the Mediterranean coast of Africa (d) In the Nile valley

539. Swaziland is encircled by South Africa except for a short boundary with one other country. Which country?

(a) Zimbabwe (b) Botswana (c) Mozambique (d) Lesotho

540. Where is the Nubian Desert?

(a) Egypt (b) Ethiopia (c) Somalia (d) Sudan

541. What is El Qahira better known as?

(a) Aswan (b) Cairo (c) Port Said (d) Alexandria

542. Of which country is Bangui the capital?

(a) Rwanda (b) Burundi (c) Central African Republic (d) Cameroon

543. What is Salisbury now called?

(a) Harare (b) Bulawayo (c) Kariba
(d) Maramba

544. What is the area of land in Egypt which is below sea level?

(a) The Nile Valley (b) Qattara Depression (c) The Aswan Reservoir (d) The Sudd

545. What is the Malagasy Republic now called?

(a) Mauritius (b) Malawi (c) Mozambique (d) Madagascar

546. Where are the Makarikari Salt Pans?

(a) Botswana (b) Zambia (c) Namibia (d) South Africa

547. Which is the capital of Togo?

(a) Lomé (b) Cotonou (c) Kumasi (d) Sokode

548. Of which country is the island of Pemba a part?

(a) Somalia (b) Kenya (c) Tanzania (d) Mozambique

549. Cape Town, Pretoria, and Bloemfonteinare South African cities with something in common. What?

(a) All gold mining centres (b) All provincial capitals (c) All cities on the coast (d) All national capitals (administrative, legislative and judicial)

550. Which mountain range stretches across Algeria and Morocco?

(a) Atlas Mountains (b) Soda Mountains (c) El Rif Mountains (d) The Erg Ranges

551. Which is the capital of Cameroon?

(a) Douala (b) Yaoundé (c) Brazzaville (d) Libréville

552. Which countries share the waters of Lake Kariba?

94

(a) Malawi and Zambia (b) Zimbabwe and Botswana (c) Zambia and Zimbabwe (d) Zimbabwe and Mozambique

553. What is Kimberley famous for?

(a) Diamonds (b) Oil (c) Gold (d) Iron

554. Which island nation lies between Madagascar and the African mainland?

(a) Mauritius (b) Zanzibar (c) Seychelles (d) The Comoros

555. What is the Belgian Congo called today?

(a) Congo (b) Zaire (c) Benin (d) Burkina Faso

556. What are the historical names of the four stretches of coast from Liberia to Nigeria?

(a) Grain Coast, Ivory Coast, Gold Coast and Slave Coast (b) Mountainous Coast, Free Coast, Ivory Coast and Gold Coast (c) Sierra Coast, Ghana Coast, Benin Coast, Niger Coast (d) Palmas Coast, Volta Coast, Benin Coast, Bonny Coast

557. Which African city finds a prominent place in the battle song of the US Marines?

(a) Alexandria (b) Tripoli (c) Tangier (d) Tunis

558. What is Africa's westernmost major city?

(a) Banjul (b) Casablanca (c) Dakar (d) Nouakchott

559. Where is Swahili generally spoken?

(a) West Africa (b) Moorish Africa (c) South Africa (d) East Africa

560. How many lakes are a part of Zaire's eastern borders?

(a) Five (b) Three (c) Six (d) Two

561. What are the names of the Spanish enclaves in North Africa?

(a) Tangier and Oran (b) Ceuta and Melilla (c) Tenerife and Las Palmas (d) Tangier and Gibraltar

562. Which two South African provinces take their names from rivers?

(a) Orange Free State & Transvaal (b) Cape and Transvaal (c) Natal and Orange (d) Cape and Natal

563. Which is the capital of the country that used to be called Abyssinia?

(a) Asmara (b) Massawa (c) Mogadiscio (d) Addis Ababa

564. In which country is the Kalahari Desert?

(a) South Africa (b) Namibia (c) Botswana (d) Angola

565. What was Burkina Faso previously called?

(a) Upper Volta (b) Dahomey (c) Liberia (d) Gabon

566. What is Saharwi?

(a) The Sahara Desert (b) The name Western Sahara has been given by those seeking its independence (c) A desert wind in the Sahara (d) The desert region of Mauritania

567. What is the name of the Angolan enclave sandwiched by Zaire and Congo?

(a) Cabinda (b) Pagalu (c) Bioko (d) Principé

568. Near which well-known coastal physical feature is Cape Town?

(a) Cape Agulhas (b) The Cape of Good Hope (c) Cape St Francis (d) St Helena Bay

569. Which country is entirely surrounded by Senegal, except for a narrow coastal strip?

(a) Sierra Leone (b) Guinea (c) Liberia (d) Gambia

570. Which was the former capital and, at present, the biggest city of Tanzania?

(a) Mwanza (b) Zanzibar (c) Dar-es-Salam (d) Kigoma

571. What does South Africa's mineral wealth mainly comprise?

(a) Gold and Diamonds (b) Oil and Iron (c) Copper and Nickel (d) Uranium and Tungsten

572. Where are the Victoria Falls?

(a) Malawi-Zambia border (b) Zambia-Zimbabwe border (c) Zimbabwe-Botswana border (d) Zambia-Tanzania border

573. Of which country or territory is St Denis the chief town?

(a) Mauritius (b) Comoro (c) Reunion (d) Seychelles

574. Which city lies in the confluence of the two main branches of the River Nile?

(a) Aswan (b) Khartoum (c) Asyut (d) Cairo

575. Zambia and Zimbabwe had a common territorial name when they were administered by Britain. What was this name?

(a) Southwest Africa (b) Tanganyika (c) Nyasaland (d) Rhodesia (North and South)

576. Of which country is Cyrenaica a part?

(a) Libya (b) Egypt (c) Algeria (d) Morocco

577. Which former Italian colony was integrated with Ethiopia in 1952?

(a) Somalia (b) Eritrea (c) Libya (d) Djibouti

578. In which countries are there cities commemorating in their names Stanley and Livingstone?

(a) Tanzania and Burundi (b) Congo and Central African Republic (c) Zaire and Zambia (d) Zimbabwe and Rwanda

579. In which county is Lambarene, where Dr. Schweitzer lived?

(a) Gabon (b) Equatorial Guinea (c) Congo (d) Cameroon

580. Which are the towns at the either end of the Suez Canal?

(a) Cairo and Aswan (b) Port Said and Suez (c) Alexandria and Cairo (d) Ismailia and Asyut

581. Which country was once called Dahomey?

(a) Togo (b) Ghana (c) Benin (d) Gabon

582. Of whose empire was Zaire once a part?

(a) Britain's (b) France's (c) Germany's (d) Belgium's

583. Which is the highest peak in Africa?

(a) Mt. Kilimanjaro (b) Mt. Ruwenzori (c) Mt. Kenya (d) Ras Dashan

584. Which major city developed as a consequence of the boom in the Witwatersrand?

(a) Pretoria (b) Johannesburg (c) Ladysmith (d) Bloemfontein

585. Which is the northernmost city in Africa?

(a) Algeria (b) Tunis (c) Bizerte (d) Tangier

586. What is the name of the lake the Aswan High Dam has helped create?

(a) Lake Luxor (b) Lake Aswan (c) Lake Thebes (d) Lake Nasser

587. Which is the longest African river emptying into the Indian Ocean?

(a) The Zambezi (b) The Nile (c) The Shibeli (d) The Juba

588. Which northern Nigerian city is the centre on which the major caravan routes converge?

(a) Kaduna (b) Jas (c) Kano (d) Nguru

589. Which is the country that is broadly divided into Ovamboland, Damaraland and Great Namaland?

(a) Angola (b) Namibia (c) Zaire (d) Botswana

590. Which was the largest of the French West African countries in area?

(a) Mauritania (b) Niger (c) Burkina Faso (d) Mali

591. Which three mainland African nations did Portugal once rule?

(a) Guinea-Bissau, Angola and Mozambique
(b) Guinea, Sierra Leone, and Ivory Coast
(c) Equatorial Guinea, Gabon, and Cameroon
(d) Ghana, Benin, and Togo

592. Which is the biggest city in Natal?

(a) Pietemaritzburg (b) Durban (c) Ladysmith (d) East London

593. Lake Chad is, of course, in Chad. But which countries does it seasonally extend into?

(a) Central African Republic and Sudan (b) Libya and Niger (c) Niger, Nigeria, and Cameroon (d) Cameroon, Central African Republic, and Sudan

594. A part of Namibia is a finger pointing eastwards. What is this territory called?

(a) The Caprivi Strip (b) The Zambezi Valley (c) The Angola Range (d) The Botswana Ridge

595. Which African city was once an internationally administered enclave?

(a) Casablanca (b) Tangier (c) Marrakesh (d) Oran

596. Through which country does the greater part of the Nile flow?

(a) Egypt (b) Ethiopia (c) Chad (d) Sudan

597. Conakry and Abidjan are capitals of countries which are connected in many ways. What is the physical connection and the erstwhile political connection?

(a) Both have a common border and were once part of French West Africa (b) Both were once one country of ancient lineage (c) Both were once British possessions with a common border (d) Both are narrow landmasses that once were part of two other countries

598. After which American President is the capital of an African country named?

(a) Lincoln (b) Monroe (c) Jefferson (d) Buchanan

599. On which river is Brazzaville?

(a) Zaire (b) Niger (c) Congo (d) Kasai

600. Where are the Craters of the Moon?

(a) Mt. Kilimanjaro (b) Mt. Kenya (c) Ras Dashan (d) Mt. Ruwenzori

IX

EUROPE

Including
European Russia
and the islands
off the coasts
of the continent

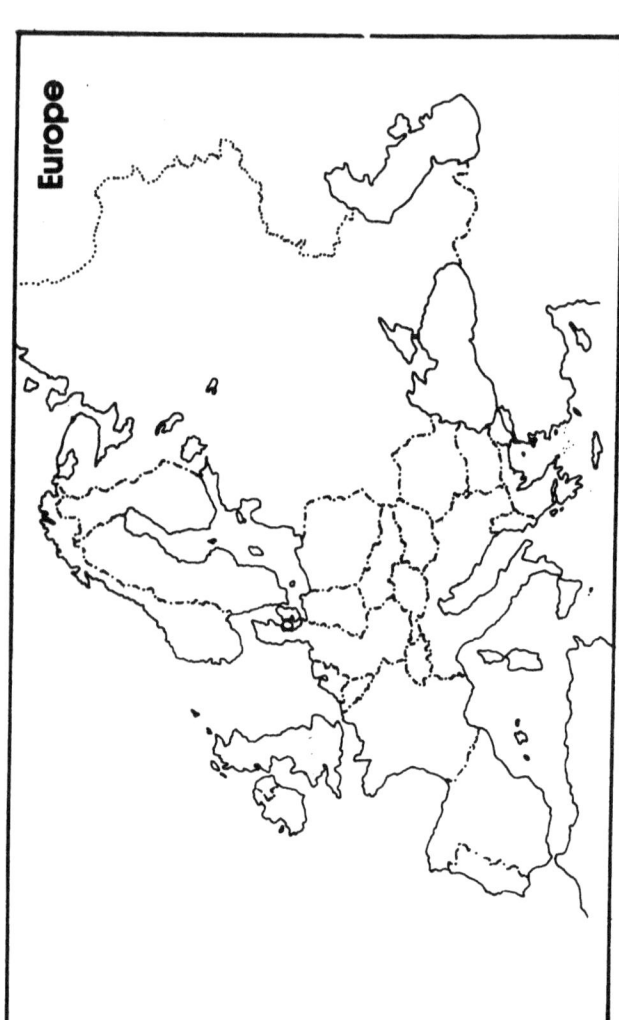
Europe

601. Where exactly is Gallipoli?

(a) Between Crete and Rhodes (b) European Turkey, overlooking the Dardanelles (c) In the Dodecanese islands (d) A peninsula in eastern Greece

602. Which is Poland's major port?

(a) Gdansk (b) Gdynia (c) Szozecin (d) Rostock

603. Of which country is Brittany a part?

(a) Britain (b) Ireland (c) France (d) Belgium

604. What important port is on the White Sea?

(a) Murmansk (b) Arkhangelsk (c) Kara (d) Karaul

605. Where is Bonn and what is its significance?

(a) An industrial city in the Ruhr (b) A historic city in Western Germany (c) A holiday resort in Germany (d) It was the capital of the Federal Republic of Germany (West Germany) before the two Germanys united

606. In which mountain range is Andorra?

(a) Pyrennes (b) Alps (c) Vosges (d) Jura

607. What is Russia's northernmost major port?

(a) Arkhangelsk (b) Murmansk (c) Kara (d) Nordvik

608. In which country is Serbia?

(a) Yugoslavia (b) Greece (c) Italy (d) Albania

609. What important mineral wealth do Romania and Russia have in common?

(a) Gold (b) Iron ore (c) Oil (d) Copper

610. Of what country is Berne the capital?

(a) Austria (b) Monaco (c) Germany (d) Switzerland

611. What used to be the correct name of the Russian portion of the erstwhile USSR?

(a) The Russian Republic (b) The Russian Soviet Federal Socialist Republic (c) The Soviet Russian Republic (d) The Russian Federal Republic

612. With what activity is the Dogger Bank associated?

(a) Fishing (b) Oil drilling (c) Undersea mining (d) The Chunnel

613. Where is Transylvania?

(a) Bulgaria (b) Yugoslavia (c) Romania (d) Hungary

614. Which major port in southern Russia is an important centre of the oil industry?

(a) Astrakhan (b) Groznyy (c) Baku (d) Tbilsi

615. Which countries' separate entities are part of the Iberian peninsula?

(a) Portugal, Spain, Andorra, and Gibraltar (b) Portugal, Spain, Minorca (c) Portugal and Spain (d) Portugal, Spain, Majorca

616. Which countries does the Gulf of Bothnia separate?

(a) Sweden and Estonia (b) Finland and Estonia (c) Sweden and Poland (d) Sweden and Finland

617. What was Voroshilovgrad known as until recently?

(a) Leningrad (b) Stalingrad (c) Volgograd (d) Kaliningrad

618. In which country or countries is Lapland?

(a) USSR and Finland (b) Finland (c) Sweden and Finland (d) Norway, Sweden, and Finland

619. What are the two major industrial cities in northern Italy?

(a) Milan and Turin (b) Genoa and Turin (c) Genoa and Trieste (d) Milan and Bologna

620. What is the British portion of Ireland colloquially called?

(a) Belfast (b) Ulster (c) Northern Ireland (d) British Ireland

621. What do Lesvos, Rhodes, Khios, and Samos have in common?

(a) All are Greek towns (b) All are claimed by Turkey (c) All are islands off Greece (d) All are Aegean islands

622. What is Eire better known as?

(a) Ireland (b) Ulster (c) Northern Ireland (d) Irish Republic

623. What geographical feature do Romania, Bulgaria and European Turkey have in common?

(a) The Carpathian Mountains (b) The River Danube (c) A Black Sea coast (d) A Slav heritage

624. Across which river do the Black Forest and the Vosges face each other?

(a) The Rhone (b) The Danube (c) The Seine (d) The Rhine

625. Which is the largest inland water body in Europe?

(a) The Caspian Sea (b) Aral Sea (c) Lake Leman (d) Lake Constance

626. With what country or countries does Monaco have borders?

(a) France and Spain (b) France and Italy
(c) Only France (d) Only Italy

627. Which territory is the southernmost part of Europe?

(a) Malta (b) Gibraltar (c) Crete (d) Rhodes

628. To whom do the Faeroe Islands belong?

(a) Britain (b) Norway (c) Sweden (d) Denmark

629. Which is the sea which laps the greater part of Albania's coast?

(a) Ionian Sea (b) Aegean Sea (c) Adriatic Sea
(d) Tyrrhenian Sea

630. In which Russian republic are the Pripyat Marshes?

(a) Byelorussia (b) Russia (c) Ukraine
(d) Moldavia

631. Which is the longest river in Italy?

(a) Serio (b) Po (c) Tiber (d) Arno

632. What is Ploesti famous for?

(a) Marble (b) Orchards (c) Iron Ore (d) Oil

633. How many independent principalities are there in Europe?

(a) Seven (b) Five (c) Six (d) Four

634. Which countries does the Skagerrak separate?

(a) Norway and Denmark (b) Denmark and
Sweden (c) Sweden and Finland (d) Germany
and Denmark

635. In which part of the world would you find the Basques?

(a) Belgium (b) Southern Spain (c) Southern
France (d) Northeast Spain

636. What geographical feature do Estonia, Latvia, and Lithuania have in common?

(a) A Baltic coast (b) All face the Gulf of Finland (c) All their capitals are ports (d) The Drina flows through them

637. Which sea separates Britain from Scandinavia?

(a) English Channel (b) The North Sea (c) Arctic Ocean (d) Skagerrak

638. Which Russian peninsula juts into the Black Sea?

(a) Balaklava (b) Yalta (c) Crimea (d) Sevastapol

639. What is the name of the area in Germany where there is the greatest concentration of heavy industry?

(a) The Rhine (b) The Ruhr (c) Heligoland (d) Westphalia

640. Which is the chief city of Wales?

(a) Swansea (b) Cardiff (c) Llanelli (d) Newport

641. World War I, it is stated, had its beginnings in Sarajevo. In which country is Sarajevo today?

(a) Poland (b) Hungary (c) Austria (d) Yugoslavia

642. Which British territory is part of Continental Europe?

(a) Calais (b) Gibraltar (c) Jersey (d) Guernsey

643. What are the crossing points at the narrowest portion of the English Channel?

(a) Portsmouth and Le Havre (b) Weymouth and Cherbourg (c) Dover and Calais (d) Folkstone and Boulogne

644. Across which countries do the Alps stretch?

(a) France, Switzerland, and Italy with bits in Germany and Yugoslavia (b) France, Switzerland, and Germany (c) France and Italy (d) Switzerland, Italy, Germany, and Yugoslavia

645. On which river is Paris?

(a) Seine (b) Loire (c) Somme (d) Garonne

646. Overlooking which water-body is Edinburgh?

(a) Firth of Clyde (b) St Andrew's Bay (c) Firth of Forth (d) North Sea

647. Of which country is the island of Sardinia a part?

(a) Malta (b) Spain (c) France (d) Italy

648. Which countries combine to form the United Kingdom?

(a) England, Scotland, Wales, and Northern Ireland (b) England, Scotland, and Wales (c) England and Northern Ireland (d) England, Scotland, and Britain

649. Which is the chief town of a Baltic territory the USSR claimed from the Poles?

(a) Kaunas (b) Kaliningrad (c) Vilnius (d) Riga

650. Malta mainly comprises two islands. What is the smaller island called?

(a) Gozo (b) Elba (c) Lampedusa (d) Pantelleria

651. What is Geneva's lake known as?

(a) Lake Como (b) Lake Neuchatel (c) Lake Leman (d) Lake Constance

652. Which are the Benelux countries?

(a) Belgium, Netherlands, and Luxembourg (b) France, Belgium, and Netherlands (c) Bel-

gium and Luxembourg (d) Belgium and Netherlands

653. Which French province is an island?

(a) Majorca (b) Corsica (c) Minorca
(d) Copenhagen

654. Which country has territory on all sides of the
Aegean Sea?

(a) Bulgaria (b) Yugoslavia (c) Greece
(d) Turkey

655. Which capital is on the eastern end of an island
that is almost the furthest point from the
country's mainland?

(a) Stockholm (b) Athens (c) Tirana
(d) Copenhagen

656. Into which sea does the Danube flow?

(a) The Black Sea (b) Aegean Sea (c) Sea of
Marmara (d) Adriatic Sea

657. Which are the main Channel Islands?

(a) Alderney and Jersey (b) Jersey and
Guernsey (c) Shetlands and Guernsey
(d) Alderney and Shetlands

658. Which countries have stretches of the Riviera
coast?

(a) Italy and France (b) France alone (c) Italy,
Monaco, and France (d) Monaco and Italy

659. Which is North Italy's great port?

(a) Genoa (b) Trieste (c) Venice (d) La
Spezia

660. Which is the southernmost federal unit of
Yugoslavia?

(a) Montenegro (b) Croatia (c) Serbia
(d) Macedonia

661. Where exactly is Loch Ness?

(a) North-east Scotland (b) West England (c) Northern Ireland (d) Between Ireland and Scotland

662. Where is Mount Olympus?

(a) Albania (b) Greece (c) Hungary (d) Yugoslavia

663. What is (European) Russia's longest river?

(a) Dniester (b) Dnieper (c) Don (d) Volga

664. Which is the effective (administrative) capital of the Netherlands?

(a) Amsterdam (b) The Hague (c) Rotterdam (d) Eindhoven

665. What are the south-eastern nations of Europe called?

(a) The Balkan nations (b) The Baltic nations (c) The Mediterannean nations (d) The Latin nations

666. In which country is Flanders?

(a) France (b) Denmark (c) The Netherlands (d) Belgium

667. Which is Russia's biggest Black Sea port?

(a) Rostov (b) Sevastopol (c) Odessa (d) Sochi

668. Which is the northernmost important city in Sweden?

(a) Lulea (b) Narvik (c) Tromso (d) Kiruna

669. On which river is Hamburg?

(a) Oder (b) Elbe (c) Rhine (d) Weser

670. Where exactly is Andalusia?

(a) Southern Spain (b) Portugal (c) Northern Italy (d) Western France

671. Near which city is Versailles?

(a) Rouen (b) Marseilles (c) Paris (d) Rheims

672. Where exactly is Ruthenia?

(a) A part of western Russia (b) The Hungary-Romania border region (c) Eastern Czechoslovakia (d) Where the erstwhile USSR meets Czechoslovakia and Hungary

673. Which Belgian port is connected to the UK by a ferry service?

(a) Antwerp (b) Ostend (c) Vlissingen (d) Bruges

674. What are the two largest cities north of the Cheviot Hills?

(a) Glasgow and Edinburgh (b) Edinburgh and Dundee (c) Glasgow and Dundee (d) Aberdeen and Glasgow

675. What is Petrograd and St Petersburg known as today?

(a) Moscow (b) Leningrad (c) Kiev (d) Volgograd

676. Where exactly is the Isle of Man?

(a) Between Britain and Northern Ireland (b) Between Britain and France (c) North-east of Britain (d) North-west of Britain

677. In which country is the Matterhorn?

(a) Germany (b) France (c) Italy (d) Switzerland

678. Where exactly is County Limerick?

(a) Ulster (b) Southern Ireland (c) Wales (d) Southern England

679. Which countries does the Simplon Pass connect?

(a) France and Switzerland (b) Austria and Switzerland (c) Switzerland and Italy (d) France and Italy

680. Which Russian republic or republics border Iran?

(a) Armenia, Azerbaijan, and Turkmen (b) Georgia and Armenia (c) Uzbek, Georgia, and Azerbaijan (d) Uzbek and Turkmen

681. Where is Innsbruck?

(a) Germany (b) Austria (c) Switzerland (d) Hungary

682. Which country or countries does European Turkey border?

(a) Bulgaria and Romania (b) The erstwhile USSR (c) Greece alone (d) Bulgaria and Greece

683. Which is the great port in the south of France?

(a) Nice (b) Marseilles (c) Cannes (d) Toulon

684. Of which country is Budapest the capital?

(a) Hungary (b) Romania (c) Austria (d) Bulgaria

685. Which capital is also known as Helsingfors?

(a) Stockholm (b) Helsinki (c) Oslo (d) Reykjavik

686. What is the Hellespont of legend now known as?

(a) The Bosphorous (b) The Straits of Gibraltar (c) The Dardanelles (d) The Straits of Messina

687. What is the highest mountain in Europe outside the erstwhile USSR?

(a) Vesuvius (b) Mont Blanc (c) Olympus (d) Matterhorn

688. In which country or countries are the Jura Mountains?

(a) Switzerland and Austria (b) Germany (c) Austria and Switzerland (d) France and Switzerland

689. What is the "ball" the Italian toe appears ready to boot?

(a) Sicily (b) Elba (c) Sardinia (d) Pantellaria

690. In which country is the Kiel Canal?

(a) Denmark (b) Germany (c) Holland (d) France

691. What is the mountainous spine of Italy called?

(a) The Apennines (b) Auvergne Range (c) Pennine Alps (d) Grand Massif

692. What is another name for the Western Isles?

(a) The Shetlands (b) The Channel Islands (c) The Hebrides (d) The Irish Isles

693. Which river partly forms the border between Germany and Poland?

(a) Elbe (b) Oder (c) Vistula (d) Saale

694. To whom do the Ionian Islands belong?

(a) Albania (b) Bulgaria (c) Turkey (d) Greece

695. What are the northernmost British islands?

(a) The Shetlands (b) The Hebrides (c) The Orkneys (d) Skye

696. Which major Italian port-city neighbours Yugoslavia?

(a) Venice (b) Trieste (c) Bari (d) Taranto

697. Which is the capital of Georgia?

(a) Groznyy (b) Yerevan (c) Baku (d) Tbilisi

698. Where are Piedmont and Lombardy?

(a) Italy (b) Austria (c) France (d) Switzerland

699. Where exactly is the Black Forest?

(a) Western Austria (b) Eastern Switzerland
(c) South-western corner of Germany
(d) Along the Austria-Germany border.

700. In which country is the Rhone?

(a) Germany (b) France (c) Italy (d) Switzerland

X

NORTH AMERICA
AND THE CARIBBEAN

Including the
islands of
the Caribbean and
the countries of
Central America
up to the southern
borders of Panama

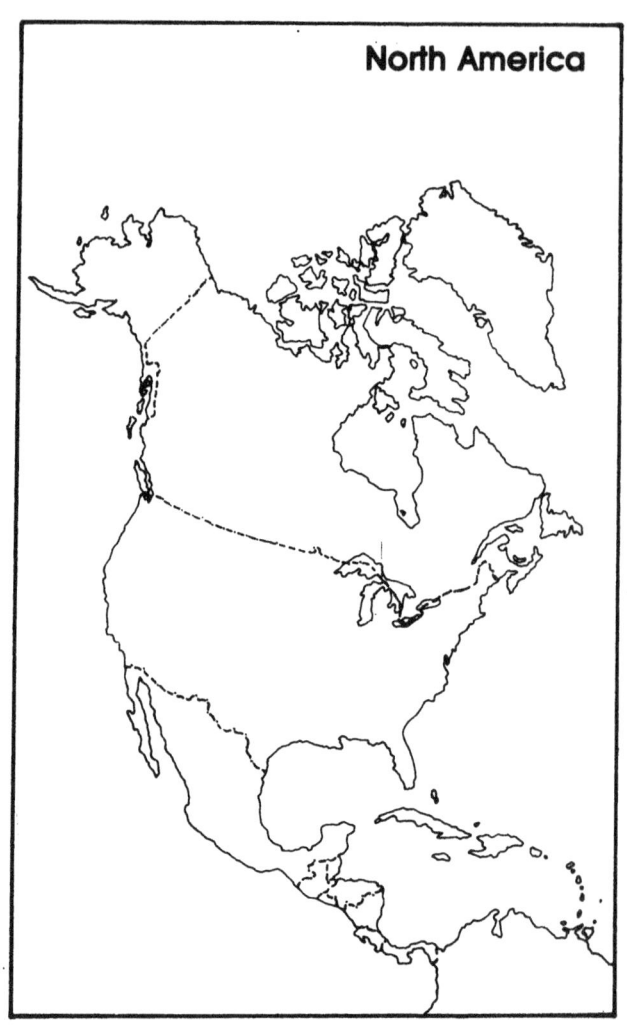

North America

701. In which state in the USA would you find Rome and Athens?

(a) Alabama (b) South Carolina (c) Georgia (d) Tennessee

702. Where are the Everglades in the USA?

(a) Florida (b) Georgia (c) Louisiana (d) Mississippi

703. To which does Greenland belong?

(a) Iceland (b) Canada (c) USA (d) Denmark

704. Where is Death Valley in the USA?

(a) Nevada (b) California (c) Arizona (d) Utah

705. Which cities mark the two ends of the Panama Canal?

(a) Santiago and Panama City (b) Colon and Santiago (c) Chitre and La Chorrera (d) Colon and Panama City

706. What is the westernmost American territory in North America?

(a) Attu Island (b) Kodiak Island (c) St Lawrence Island (d) Trinity Island

707. In which state is Washington, the American capital?

(a) Washington State (b) New York State (c) The Federal District of Columbia (d) Maryland State

708. Which is the capital of Florida?

(a) Tallahassee (b) Miami (c) Tampa (d) Jacksonville

709. Where exactly is the Isthmus of Tehuantepec?

(a) Southern Panama (b) Southern Mexico (c) Southern Guatemala (d) Southern Costa Rica

710. What is Cape Kennedy now known as?

(a) Cape St George (b) Cape Sable (c) Cape Canaveral (d) Cape Romano

711. Which is Canada's westernmost province?

(a) British Columbia (b) Northwest Territory (c) Alberta (d) Yukon

712. What is the Yucatan?

(a) A peninsular state in Mexico (b) A mountainous region in Mexico (c) A Guatemalan enclave in Mexico (d) A part of the USA bordering Mexico

713. What separates the USA and the erstwhile USSR?

(a) Bering Sea (b) Bering Strait (c) Norton Sound (d) Gulf of Alaska

714. What is the last remaining fragment of French-owned land in North America?

(a) Magdalen Island (b) Sept Iles (c) St Pierre & Miquelon (d) Cape Breton Island

715. The Mississippi is joined by another big river and both are often called by a joint name. What is this name?

(a) Mississippi-Missouri (b) Mississippi-Illinois (c) Mississippi-Arkansas (d) Mississippi-Tennessee

716. Which is the biggest French territory in the Caribbean?

(a) Martinique (b) Marie Galante (c) St Martin (d) Guadeloupe

717. Which is the highest volcano in North America?

(a) Citlaltepetl, Mexico (b) Popocatepetl, Mexico (c) Mt Shasta, USA (d) Mt Whitney, USA

718. Which is the largest lake entirely in Canada?

(a) Lake Winnipeg (b) Great Slave Lake (c) Great Bear Lake (d) Reindeer Lake

719. Which countries in the Caribbean share the island of Hispaniola?

(a) Cuba and Haiti (b) Cuba and Jamaica (c) The Dominican Republic and Puerto Rico (d) Haiti and the Dominican Republic

720. Which Canadian town was the boom town of the Gold Rush?

(a) Klondike (b) Dawson Creek (c) Whitehorse (d) Inayo

721. Which is the highest mountain range in the eastern United States?

(a) Alleghenies (b) Appalachians (c) Catskills (d) Cumberlands

722. Which is the biggest Canadian island?

(a) Newfoundland (b) Victoria (c) Baffin (d) Devon

723. To which does the Gulf of California belong?

(a) The USA (b) The USA and Mexico (c) Mexico and Guatemala (d) Mexico

724. On which river is the city of New York?

(a) Hudson (b) Potomac (c) Shenandoah (d) Allegheny

725. Which landmark is considered the line of separation between the North and South American continents?

(a) Yucatan (b) Panama Canal (c) Gulf of Panama (d) Isthmus of Tehuantepec

726. Which Canadian province is separated from the USA mainly by the Great Lakes?

(a) Ontario (b) Alberta (c) Manitoba (d) Quebec

727. Where exactly is the Mojave Desert?

(a) Yucatan (b) New Mexico, USA (c) North-western Mexico (d) California, USA

728. Which is the highest mountain in North America?

(a) Mount Rainier (b) Mount Logan (c) Mount Orizaba (d) Mount Whitney

729. The Gulf of Mexico is entered through two straits. What are they?

(a) Yucatan Channel and Florida Strait (b) Windward Passage and Mona Passage (c) North-west and North-east Providence Channels (d) Florida Strait and Cabot Strait

730. Which US state reflects its strong French beginnings in the names of many of its important cities?

(a) Florida (b) Texas (c) Louisiana (d) Iowa

731. Which is the largest French-speaking city in North America?

(a) Quebec (b) Montreal (c) Trois Riviere (d) Sept Iles

732. What is the Caribbean group of islands the USA and the UK share?

(a) Leeward Islands (b) Puerto Rico (c) Windward Islands (d) The Virgin Islands

733. Newfoundland and this part of mainland Canada are a single province. What is the name of this territory?

(a) Labrador (b) Baffin Island (c) Nova Scotia (d) Prince Edward Island

734. What and where is Charlotte Amalie?

(a) Capital of the French territory of Guadeloupe (b) A mountain on the French island of Martinique (c) Capital of the US Virgin Islands located on St Thomas Island (d) A beach resort in Haiti

735. Into what does the Mississippi empty?

(a) The Caribbean Sea (b) The Gulf of Mexico (c) The Atlantic Ocean (d) Galveston Bay

736. What are the major islands of the Greater Antilles?

(a) Cuba, Hispaniola, and Jamaica (b) Cuba and the Bahamas (c) Jamaica, Haiti, and Puerto Rico (d) Cuba, Haiti, and Jamaica

737. Which inland Texas city is an important port?

(a) Galveston (b) Houston (c) Corpus Christi (d) Port Arthur

738. Which great water body substantially reduces northern Canada's landmass?

(a) Labrador Sea (b) Baffin Bay (c) Hudson Bay (d) Beaufort Sea

739. Which is the smallest state in USA?

(a) Vermont (b) Maine (c) Columbia (d) Rhode Island

740. How many countries are there in the narrow neck between Mexico and the first country that's wholly in South America?

(a) Seven (b) Five (c) Three (d) Eight

741. In which country is the city of Niagara Falls?

(a) The USA (b) The Bahamas (c) Canada (d) Bermuda

742. These Caribbean nations have almost identical names. Which is the odd pair out?

(a) The Grenadines and Grenada (b) Dominica and the Dominican Republic (c) Barbuda and Barbados (d) St Martin and Martinique

743. To which political island grouping does Curacao belong?

(a) The French West Indies (b) The Bahamas (c) The Cayman Islands (d) The Netherlands Antilles

744. Which great city is on the shores of Lake Michigan?

(a) Milwaukee (b) Gary (c) Chicago (d) Evanston

745. What is the Caribbean island of St Christopher better known as?

(a) St Kitts (b) St Croix (c) Curacao (d) Caicos

746. Where exactly is the Grand Canyon?

(a) Texas, USA (b) Arizona, USA (c) Montana, USA (d) Yukon, Canada

747. What is the largest province in Canada?

(a) The Northwest Territories (b) British Columbia (c) Newfoundland (d) Quebec

748. In which group of islands is Montserrat?

(a) Windward Islands (b) Trinidad and Tobago (c) Leeward Islands (d) The Bahamas

749. One of the Great Lakes is wholly in the USA Which one?

(a) Lake Superior (b) Lake Erie (c) Lake Huron (d) Lake Michigan

750. Which is the capital of Canada?

(a) Ottawa (b) Toronto (c) Montreal (d) St John's

751. Where exactly in the USA is Yellowstone National Park?

(a) Utah (b) Wyoming (c) Montana (d) Nevada

752. Which province of Canada is an island?

(a) Newfoundland (b) British Columbia (c) Prince Edward (d) Nova Scotia

753. What is the capital of the Bahamas?

(a) Nassau (b) Kemp's Bay (c) Matthew Town (d) New Providence

754. Which is the biggest city on Canada's west coast?

(a) Seattle (b) Portland (c) Victoria (d) Vancouver

755. Which American state is completely cut off from a substantial portion of its territory by water?

(a) Ohio (b) Michigan (c) New York (d) Wisconsin

756. Which is the biggest city (population-wise) in North America?

(a) Mexico City (b) New York City (c) Chicago (d) San Francisco

757. Where exactly is Lake Winnipeg?

(a) Northern Saskatchewan (b) Western Northwest Territories (c) Southern Manitoba (d) Southern Ontario

758. Where exactly is the Great Salt Lake?

(a) Manitoba, Canada (b) Utah, USA (c) Monterrey, Mexico (d) California, USA

759. Through which province does the greater portion of the Mackenzie Highway run?

(a) Manitoba (b) Ontario (c) British Columbia (d) Alberta

760. Of which country is Havana the capital?

(a) Cuba (b) Dominica (c) Dominican Republic (d) Puerto Rico

761. Which is the easternmost of the Caribbean islands?

(a) St Vincent (b) Tobago (c) St Lucia (d) Barbados

762. Which town in USA is closest to Havana?

(a) Key West (b) Miami (c) Palm Beach (d) Fort Lauderdale

763. Which is the capital of St Lucia?

(a) Kingston (b) Castries (c) St George's (d) Roseau

764. Several islands are part of British Columbia. Which is the biggest of them?

(a) Queen Charlotte Islands (b) Moresby Island (c) Vancouver Island (d) Graham Island

765. What do Madison and Lincoln have in common?

(a) Both are rivers in USA (b) Both are state capitals in USA (c) Both are on the Great Lakes (d) Both are towns in Ontario

766. How is the Atlantic reached from the Great Lakes?

(a) By the St Lawrence River (b) Through the Cabot Strait (c) Through the Gulf of St Lawrence (d) Through the Labrador Sea

767. What exactly is New England?

(a) The eastern provinces of Canada (b) Six north-eastern states of the USA (c) The 13 states that became the USA (d) Another name for British Columbia

768. What is the southernmost North American country if the Americans are considered as being geographically divided only into North and South America?

(a) Costa Rica (b) El Salvador (c) Nicaragua (d) Honduras

769. On what river is the American capital?

(a) The Hudson (b) The Potomac (c) The Susquehanna (d) The Delaware

770. Where is the Mosquito Coast?

(a) Honduras (b) Panama (c) Nicaragua (d) Costa Rica

771. A peninsula extending from the westernmost mainland American state is part of Mexico. What is it called?

(a) The Yucatan (b) Florida (c) Guadaljara (d) Lower, or Baja, California

772. Which territory in the Caribbean belonging to USA is described as a Commonwealth?

(a) The Virgin Islands (b) Puerto Rico (c) St Croix (d) Marquesas Keys

773. Which American state has the largest amount of area over 3000 m in height (over 10,000 ft)?

(a) Colorado (b) Washington (c) Oregon (d) Nevada

774. Which Central American country has only a Pacific coastline?

(a) Honduras (b) Guatemala (c) El Salvador (d) Belize

775. Of which Canadian province is Cape Breton Island a part?

(a) Nova Scotia (b) Prince Edward Island (c) Quebec (d) Newfoundland

776. Which is the largest American state?

(a) California (b) Alaska (c) Montana (d) Texas

777. What is the geographical name for the Windward and Leeward Islands?

(a) The Greater Antilles (b) Hispaniola (c) The Lesser Antilles (d) The Eastern Antilles

778. What is called the "Prairie Province of Canada"?

(a) British Columbia (b) Manitoba (c) Alberta (d) Saskatchewan

779. Which American state has a part of its border running through Lake Ontario?

(a) New York (b) Pennsylvania (c) Ohio (d) Michigan

780. Which is the southernmost Caribbean island?

(a) Aruba (b) Isla Margarita (c) Tobago (d) Trinidad

781. In which Canadian Province is French most spoken?

(a) Nova Scotia (b) Quebec (c) New Brunswick (d) Newfoundland

782. Which city in Missouri has a twin city in Kansas?

(a) St Joseph (b) Springfield (c) Kansas City (d) Independence

783. Which mountain range stretches almost from Alaska to Mexico?

(a) The Rocky Mountains (b) The Sierra Madre (c) The Sierra Nevada (d) Cascade Range

784. Tobago is one part of a country's name. What is the other part?

(a) Jamaica (b) Trinidad (c) Caicos (d) Anguilla

785. In which state of USA is Los Alamos?

(a) Utah (b) Arizona (c) Texas (d) New Mexico

786. What is Acadia known as today?

(a) Nova Scotia (b) New Breton Island (c) Newfoundland (d) Prince Edward Island

787. State precisely which two water bodies are linked by the Panama Canal:

(a) Gulf of Mexico and the Pacific Ocean
(b) Yucatan Channel and the Gulf of California
(c) The Caribbean Sea and the Gulf of Panama
(d) The Gulf of Panama and the Atlantic Ocean

788. Which American states are not part of the landmass of USA?

(a) Hawaii and Alaska (b) Puerto Rico and Florida (c) Maine and Oregon (d) Washington and Alaska

789. Which is St Paul's twin city?

(a) Duluth (b) Chicago (c) Milwaukee (d) Minneapolis

790. Off which American state is Grand Bahama Island?

(a) Georgia (b) Florida (c) Alabama (d) Texas

791. If you holidayed in the resort town of Acapulco, in the waters of which sea would you bathe?

(a) Gulf of California (b) Gulf of Mexico (c) The Pacific Ocean (d) Caribbean Sea

792. Which American states are separated by British Columbia?

127

(a) Alaska and Washington (b) Alaska and Oregon (c) Washington and Oregon (d) Alaska and California

793. Which Central American country has the longest length of coast?

(a) Nicaragua (b) Honduras (c) Costa Rica (d) Panama

794. If a traveller by road crosses into Mexico from San Diego, which Mexican border town will he have to pass through?

(a) Mexicali (b) Tijuana (c) Nogales (d) Ciudad Juarez

795. Which towns does the only railway line in Alaska link?

(a) Seward and Fairbanks (b) Valdez and Prudhoe Bay (c) Juneau and Anchorage (d) Anchorage and Valdez

796. Which countries does the Rio Grande separate?

(a) Panama and Costa Rica (b) Mexico and Guatemala (c) The USA and Mexico (d) Nicaragua and Honduras

797. Which two Caribbean nations have very similar-sounding capitals?

(a) Haiti and Trinidad and Tobago (b) Jamaica and St Vincent and the Grenadines (c) Cuba and the Dominican Republic (d) Martinique and Haiti

798. Which is the biggest mountain range in Mexico?

(a) Sierra Nevada (b) Sierra de Juarez (c) The Southern Sierra (d) Sierra Madre

799. Which town that takes its name after one of the Great Lakes is an important city in Pennsylvania?

(a) Erie (b) Ontario (c) Huron (d) Superior

800. Reno and Las Vegas are the best known cities of this state in USA. But what is its capital?

(a) Caliente (b) Boulder City (c) Carson City (d) Eureka

XI

SOUTH AMERICA

All the countries
below Panama and
some of the islands
of the Eastern
Pacific rim

South America

801. Which country is the biggest livestock-raiser in South America?

(a) Brazil (b) Argentina (c) Uruguay (d) Bolivia

802. Which countries share the waters of Lake Titicaca?

(a) Peru and Bolivia (b) Peru and Chile (c) Bolivia and Brazil (d) Ecuador and Colombia

803. Which country or countries do the Straits of Magellan divide?

(a) Argentina (b) Colombia (c) Chile (d) Venezuela

804. What is Brazil's largest coastal city?

(a) Salvador (b) Recife (c) Fortaleza (d) Rio de Janeiro

805. What is the southernmost physical feature of South America?

(a) Cape Horn (b) Straits of Magellan (c) Tierra del Fuego (d) Falkland Islands

806. Once there were three Guianas. Which is the one that does not reflect the earlier name?

(a) Venezuela (b) Surinam (c) Ecuador (d) Uruguay

807. Which share Tierra del Fuego?

(a) Peru and Chile (b) Argentina and Paraguay (c) Chile and Argentina (d) Bolivia and Peru

808. Which major city is the easternmost point of South America?

(a) Fortaleza (b) Natal (c) Salvador (d) Recife (Pernambuco)

809. Argentines call it the Malvinas. What do most English speakers call it?

(a) The Falklands (b) Tierra del Fuego (c) Queen Adelaide Archipelago (d) South Georgia

810. Which country is South America's biggest rubber producer?

(a) Guyana (b) Colombia (c) Brazil (d) Paraguay

811. Which countries is the Simon Bolivar Highway expected to link?

(a) Venezuela, Colombia, and Peru (b) Venezuela, Colombia, and Ecuador (c) Ecaudor, Peru, and Bolivia (d) Peru, Bolivia, and Chile

812. In which State is the Federal District of Brasilia, the capital of Brazil?

(a) Goias (b) Bahia (c) Para (d) Sao Paulo

813. After which person of Irish descent is a province of Chile named?

(a) O'Hara (b) O'Brien (c) O'Donnell (d) O'Higgins

814. Which large island territory about 1000 km from its coast does Ecuador own?

(a) Juan Fernandez Islands (b) San Felix Islands (c) Galapagos Islands (d) Malpelo Islands

815. Which part of South America is called "the driest place in the world"?

(a) The Atacama Desert, Chile (b) La Montana, Peru (c) Chiquitos Plateau, Bolivia (d) Patagonia, Argentina.

816. Which is the capital of Ecuador?

(a) Paramaribo (b) Quito (c) Guayaquil (d) Cali

817. What is the main agricultural produce of Guyana?

(a) Rubber (b) Rice (c) Sugarcane (d) Bamboo

818. Which South American country does the Tropic of Capricorn divide almost equally in two?

(a) Chile (b) Brazil (c) Argentina (d) Paraguay

819. Which is the only country in South America with an "Atlantic" and a "Pacific" coast?

(a) Venezuela (b) Colombia (c) Chile (d) Argentina

820. With which country/countries has Peru been disputing its frontiers — even to the extent of going to war over them?

(a) Ecuador (b) Brazil (c) Colombia (d) Bolivia

821. Angel Falls (979m) is said to be the highest waterfall in the world. Where is it?

(a) Brazil (b) Venezuela (c) Peru (d) Ecuador

822. Which South American country is a major producer of tin?

(a) Peru (b) Chile (c) Bolivia (d) Guyana

823. Which is the biggest city in South America?

(a) Sao Paulo (b) Rio de Janeiro (c) Buenos Aires (d) Caracas

824. Which country was once called New Granada?

(a) Peru (b) Bolivia (c) Venezuela (d) Colombia

825. Which is the capital of French Guiana?

(a) I. du Diable (b) New Amsterdam
(c) Cayenne (d) Kourou

826. Which is the largest lake in South America?

(a) Lake Maracaibo (b) Lake Titicaca (c) Lake
Poopo (d) Lake Marchiquita

827. Which South American country is a major
producer of silver?

(a) Chile (b) Peru (c) Bolivia (d) Paraguay

828. Of which country is Paramaribo the capital?

(a) Guyana (b) Ecuador (c) Venezuela
(d) Surinam

829. Much of which country comprises hundreds of
islands?

(a) Peru (b) Argentina (c) Chile (d) Venezuela

830. Which is the only Portuguese-speaking country
in South America?

(a) Brazil (b) Argentina (c) Uruguay (d) Chile

831. Which is the highest mountain in South
America?

(a) Cotopaxi (b) Aconcagua (c) Chimborazo
(d) Ojos del Salada

832. On which peak in Peru are there the remains
of a splendid Inca city?

(a) Huascaran (b) Nudo Coropuna
(c) Yerupaja (d) Machu Picchu

833. What is the great river of Brazil called?

(a) Negro (b) Sao Francisco (c) Amazon
(d) Madeira

834. Where is Mount Chimborazo?

(a) Ecuador (b) Peru (c) Bolivia (d) Colombia

835. Where is New Amsterdam?

(a) Surinam (b) French Guiana (c) Guyana (d) Venezuela

836. Which country in South America is famous for its emerald mines?

(a) Colombia (b) Bolivia (c) Venezuela (d) Ecuador

837. Which port do the two landlocked countries of South America mainly use?

(a) Lima, Peru (b) Santos, Brazil (c) Antofagasta, Chile (d) Rio de Janeiro, Brazil

838. Where does South America's longest river have its source?

(a) La Montana (b) Guiana Highlands (c) Chiquito Plateau (d) In the Andes

839. What is the capital of Uruguay?

(a) La Plata (b) Punta del Este (c) Montevideo (d) Rosario

840. Which part of South America receives the highest annual rainfall?

(a) The Brazilian coast around the mouth of the Amazon (b) Manaus in Brazil (c) The Guiana coast (d) Tierra del Fuego

841. Which port does Bolivia use in Chile?

(a) Antofagasta (b) Arica (c) Iquique (d) Mejillones

842. Which two South American countries have large East Indian population?

(a) Venezuela and Guyana (b) Guyana and French Guiana (c) Guyana and Surinam (d) Venezuela and French Guiana

843. Which is described as "the highest navigable lake in the world"?

(a) Lake Titicaca (b) Lake Maracaibo (c) Lake Mirim (d) Lake Nahuel Huapi

844. Where is infamous Medellin?

(a) Bolivia (b) Venezuela (c) Chile (d) Colombia

845. In which country is the westernmost part of South America?

(a) Peru (b) Ecuador (c) Colombia (d) Chile

846. Which is the chief Argentine city in the region known as Andina?

(a) San Juan (b) Mendoza (c) San Luis (d) San Rafael

847. Which country has the greatest share of the mountains of the Guiana Highlands?

(a) Guyana (b) French Guiana (c) Venezuela (d) Brazil

848. Which is the largest island in the estuary of the Amazon?

(a) Marajo island (b) Ilha de Maraca (c) I. du Diable (d) Ilha de Caviana

849. Which is the chief port of Chile?

(a) Concepcion (b) Valparaiso (c) Vina del Mar (d) Coquimbo

850. In which country in South America is Natal a major city?

(a) Argentina (b) Peru (c) Chile (d) Brazil

851. Which is Ecuador's best known volcano?

(a) Cotopaxi (b) Chimborazo (c) Tolina (d) Bolivia

852. Which country is divided into just two provinces — Oriental (East) and Occidental (West)?

(a) Uruguay (b) Bolivia (c) Paraguay
(d) Colombia

853. With which country does Colombia share its shortest international border?

(a) Ecuador (b) Panama (c) Brazil (d) Peru

854. Which is the highest seat of government in South America?

(a) Bogota (b) Lima (c) Quito (d) La Paz

855. Which is Venezuela's main river?

(a) Orinoco (b) Aranca (c) Essequibo
(d) Paraguay

856. Which capital is near Mount Cotopaxi?

(a) La Paz (b) Quito (c) Bogota (d) Caracas

857. Which are the two rivers that flow into the Rio de la Plata?

(a) Chubut and Chico (b) Pilcomayo and Paraguay (c) Parana and Uruguay (d) Colorado and Negro

858. Of all the capitals of the South American countries on the Pacific rim, which is the one closest to sea level?

(a) Lima (b) Montevideo (c) Georgetown
(d) Caracas

859. Apart from the Andes and ranges connected to it, what is the major mountain range in Argentina?

(a) Gran Chaco (b) Cordoba Mountains
(c) Patagonia (d) Montana

860. Why was Ecuador so named?

(a) Because the Equator passes through it
(b) Because the Equator passes through its
capital (c) Because it is equally divided by the
Equator (d) Because of its Equatorial Forests

861. What major water bodies do the Straits of
Magellan link?

(a) Gulf of San Matias and the Pacific Ocean
(b) Gulf of Penas and Gulf of San Matias
(c) The Atlantic and the Pacific (d) Gulf of
San George and Gulf of Corcovado

862. Which country is the biggest producer of oil
in South America?

(a) Guyana (b) Venezuela (c) Colombia
(d) Brazil

863. What does over a third of Uruguay's exports
comprise?

(a) Wheat (b) Oil (c) Fish and fish products
(d) Meat and other animal products

864. Which country in South America has the coldest
average temperature?

(a) Chile (b) Ecuador (c) Peru (d) Colombia
and Ecuador

865. On which river is Manaus?

(a) Branco (b) Amazon (c) Madeira
(d) Negro

866. What are the steppes and prairies of South
America called?

(a) Patagonia (b) Pampas (c) Selvas (d) Mato
Grosso

867. Which is Ecuador's chief port?

(a) Guyaquil (b) Esmeraldas (c) Manta (d) La
Libertad

868. Which is the southernmost provincial capital in Chile?

(a) Puerto Natales (b) Concepcion (c) Valdivia (d) Punta Arenas

869. What is the great plateau of Brazil called?

(a) Mato Grosso (b) Serra dos Parecis (c) Brazilian Highlands (d) Parana plateau

870. Only two countries in South America do not enjoy a coastline. One is Paraguay, which is the other?

(a) Ecuador (b) Bolivia (c) Uruguay (d) Surinam

871. Up until the 1970s, which South American country provided almost half the world's fishmeal that was used for cattle fodder?

(a) Peru (b) Chile (c) Brazil (d) Argentina

872. Which is the capital of Paraguay?

(a) Sao Paulo (b) Concepcion (c) Asuncion (d) La Paz

873. Which two Caribbean territories lie off the coast of South America?

(a) St Lucia and Grenada (b) The Caymans and Jamaica (c) Barbados and Martinique (d) The Netherland Antilles, and Trinidad and Tobago

874. What is Sucre's importance?

(a) It is the legal capital and seat of the judiciary of Bolivia (b) It is the biggest town in Bolivia (c) It is a hill resort in Bolivia (d) It is the commercial capital of Bolivia

875. To which does Easter Island, in the Pacific, belong?

(a) Peru (b) Chile (c) Ecuador (d) Colombia

876. Which is the most urbanised Latin American nation?

(a) Uruguay (b) Paraguay (c) Venezuela
(d) Colombia

877. As part of a border settlement, from which country did Peru get its Tacna province?

(a) Ecuador (b) Colombia (c) Bolivia
(d) Chile

878. Which mountain range stretches from Venezuela to Southern Chile?

(a) Cordoba (b) Andes (c) La Montana
(d) Brazilian Highlands

879. Which river divides Paraguay into its two distinct halves?

(a) Paraguay (b) Parana (c) Pilcomayo
(d) Salado

880. In which country does the Amazon have its source?

(a) Colombia (b) Brazil (c) Peru (d) Bolivia

881. Which South Atlantic island/islands were, until 1985, dependencies of a British territory near Argentina?

(a) South Shetlands (b) South Orkneys
(c) Deception and Elephant Islands (d) South Georgia and South Sandwich

882. Which South American country has had a negative population growth rate in the second half of this century?

(a) Guyana, because of emigration to Britain
(b) Surinam, because of emigration to Holland,
(c) French Guiana, because of emigration to France (d) Colombia, because of the drug wars

883. Of which is Stanley the capital?

(a) The Falklands (b) South Georgia (c) South Sandwich (d) Uruguay

884. To whom do the Juan Fernandez Islands belong?

(a) Peru (b) Ecuador (c) Chile (d) Colombia

885. Which major cities straddle the Rio de la Plata?

(a) La Plata and Montevideo (b) Avellaneda and San Jose de Mayo (c) Montevideo and La Plata (d) Montevideo and Buenos Aires

886. Which country was Spain's principal vice-royalty in South America?

(a) Peru (b) Chile (c) Venezuela (d) Bolivia

887. Before Brasilia became the capital of Brazil in 1960, which was the country's capital?

(a) Rio de Janeiro (b) Sao Paulo (c) Recife (d) Salvador

888. On which river is Georgetown?

(a) Essequibo (b) Caroni (c) Berbice (d) Orinoco

889. In which country is the llama reared for its wool?

(a) Peru (b) Chile (c) Uruguay (d) Paraguay

890. What is the major mineral export of Chile?

(a) Silver (b) Tin (c) Emeralds (d) Copper

891. In which country would you find the Madeira and the Negro?

(a) Argentina (b) Brazil (c) Peru (d) Bolivia

892. Which is the capital of Chile?

(a) Santiago (b) Valparaiso (c) Concepcion (d) Antofagasta

893. Which island country is almost a part of the delta of a major South American river?

(a) Netherlands Antilles (b) Grenada (c) Trinidad and Tobago (d) Jamaica

894. Which river is shared by Argentina, Paraguay, and Brazil?

(a) Amazon (b) Madeira (c) Paraguay (d) Parana

895. Which is the stormiest part of South America?

(a) The Falkland Islands (b) The southernmost part of Chile (c) The Venezuela coast (d) Around Recife in Brazil

896. Where exactly is Devil's Island?

(a) Off the coast of French Guiana (b) Off the coast of Surinam (c) Off the coast of Guyana (d) Off the coast of Venezuela

897. After which intrepid navigator is the largest Chilean province named?

(a) Columbus (b) Vasco da Gama (c) Magellan (d) Cabot

898. Where is Porto Presidente Stroessner, a town named after the country's President?

(a) Uruguay (b) Bolivia (c) Argentina (d) Paraguay

899. What is Argentina's desert called?

(a) Pampas (b) Patagonia (c) Gran Chaco (d) Cordoba

900. What is the chief mineral produce of Guyana?

(a) Bauxite (b) Limestone (c) Tin (d) Oil

XII

AUSTRALASIA AND ANTARCTICA

Including Australia
New Zealand
the islands of
Oceania, and
Antarctica

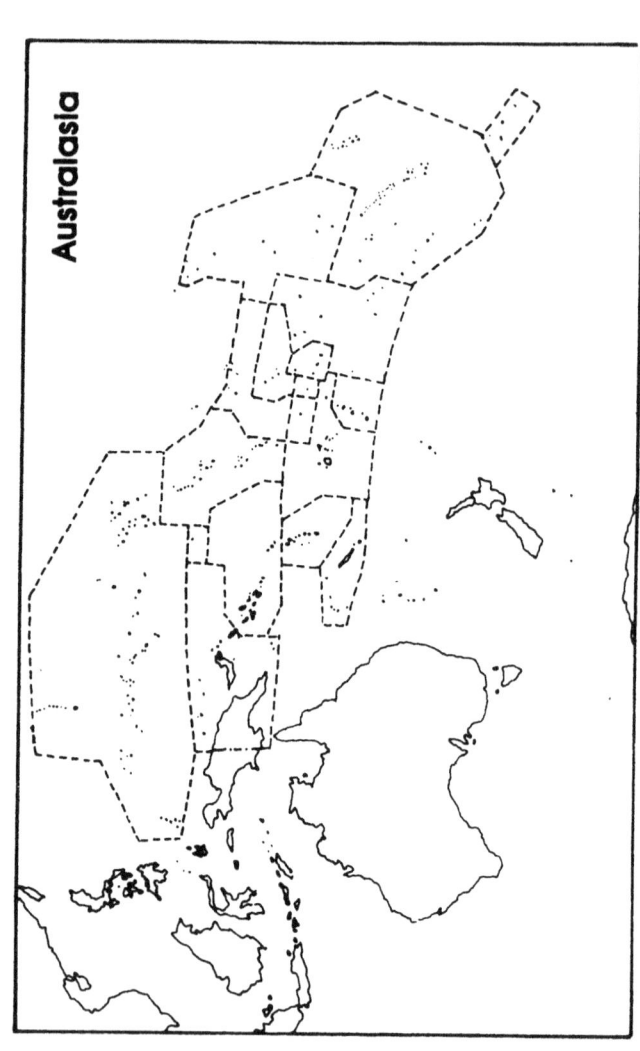

Australasia

901. What and where is Ayer's Rock?

(a) A mountain in Southern New Zealand (b) A town in Western Australia (c) A peak in Antarctica (d) An isolated rock formation which rises above the desert in Central Australia

902. Which is the world's biggest coral reef?

(a) The Great Barrier Reef (b) The Lord Howe Rise (c) The Norfolk Ridge (d) The Emperor Seamount Chain

903. With which country do you associate natural hot springs and geysers?

(a) Tonga (b) New Zealand (c) Fiji (d) Western Samoa

904. Which is the capital of Australia's Northern Territory?

(a) Darwin (b) Alice Springs (c) Birdum (d) Victoria River Downs

905. Of which country is the Bismarck Archipelago a part?

(a) Vanuatu (b) Fiji (c) Papua New Guinea (d) Solomon Islands

906. What and where is the highest mountain in Australasia?

(a) Mt. Ossa in Tasmania (b) Mt. Kosciusko in New South Wales (c) Mt. Victoria in Papua New Guinea (d) Mt. Cook in New Zealand

907. Is Guam an independent country? If not, which country administers it?

(a) No, USA (b) Yes (c) No, Australia (d) No, the Philippines

908. What separates the two main islands of New Zealand?

(a) Bass Strait (b) Cook Strait (c) Foveaux Strait (d) Torres Strait

909. What is the southernmost Australian state?

(a) Victoria (b) South Australia (c) Tasmania (d) Western Australia

910. Which independent country in the region has one of the richest per-capita-income populations in the world entirely because of its phosphate wealth?

(a) Vanuatu (b) Kiribati (c) Belau (d) Nauru

911. Of which is Suva the capital?

(a) Fiji (b) Tonga (c) Western Samoa (d) Tuvalu

912. What was Tuvalu called until Independence?

(a) Gilbert Islands (b) Ellice Islands (c) Line Islands (d) Phoenix Islands

913. Of which country are New Britain and New Ireland a part?

(a) Soloman Islands (b) New Caledonia (c) Papua New Guinea (d) Marshall Islands

914. What do these three names have in common: Victoria, Gibson, and Sandy?

(a) All deserts in Australia (b) All mountain peaks in New Zealand (c) All rivers in Papua New Guinea (d) All islands in the Solomons

915. Which Australian state capital is the furthest east?

(a) Melbourne (b) Sydney (c) Adelaide (d) Brisbane

916. What do Yap, Kosrae, Truk, and Ponape have in common?

(a) All rivers in Papua New Guinea (b) All island groups in the Federated States of Micronesia (c) All islands in French Polynesia (d) All Maori names for towns in New Zealand

917. This Australian state is an island? What is its capital?

(a) Hobart (b) Launceston (c) Geelong (d) Wagga Wagga

918. What is the capital of the Commonwealth of the Northern Marianas?

(a) Midway (b) Bougainville (c) Saipan (d) Guam

919. Whose dependency is Queen Maud Land?

(a) Sweden's (b) Norway's (c) Britain's (d) Australia's

920. What is the name of the southern plain that comes down to the Great Australian Bight?

(a) Darling Downs (b) Riverina (c) Southland (d) Nullabor Plain

921. Where exactly in Australasia would you find Coromandel?

(a) North Island, New Zealand (b) Western Australia (c) Australia's Northern Territory (d) Fiji

922. Where exactly is Mount Erebus?

(a) South Island, New Zealand (b) The Ross Dependency, Antarctica (c) The Australian Alps (d) In the Owen Stanley Range

923. Which Australian state has large areas that are marshy lakes?

(a) West Australia (b) Queensland (c) Victoria (d) South Australia

924. In which country would you find the Owen Stanley Range?

(a) Australia (b) New Zealand (c) Papua New Guinea (d) Solomon Islands

925. Where is the Seat of Government on American Samoa?

(a) Fagatogo (b) Pago Pago (c) Apia (d) Tarawa

926. New Zealand administers two self-governing Polynesian territories. Which are they?

(a) Tuvalu and Kiribati (b) Niue and Cook Islands (c) Viti Levu and Vanua Levu (d) Phoenix and Line Islands

927. Which Australian state enjoys a tropical climate?

(a) Queensland (b) Northern Territory (c) Western Australia (d) South Australia

928. What was Vanuatu once called?

(a) Line Islands (b) Gilbert Islands (c) New Hebrides (d) Loyalty Islands

929. Which large island, which is geographically part of the Solomon Islands, is politically part of Papua New Guinea?

(a) New Britain (b) Bougainville (c) Guadalcanal (d) New Ireland

930. Tasmania is to Australia as —— is to New Zealand.

(a) Great Barrier Island (b) Three Kings Island (c) Stewart Island (d) D'Urville Island

931. Which crop is under the largest acreage in Australia?

(a) Wheat (b) Rice (c) Millet (d) Sugarcane

932. Where exactly is the Canterbury Plain?

(a) New South Wales, Australia (b) North Island, New Zealand (c) South Australia (d) South Island, New Zealand

933. What are the names of the two major islands that constitute Fiji?

(a) Espiritu Santo and Malekula (b) Vanna Levu and Vita Levu (c) Melaita and Ulawa (d) Bora Bora and Rapa

934. What is Perth's port?

(a) Geraldton (b) Carnarvon (c) Fremantle (d) Albany

935. Which is the longest river in Australia?

(a) Murray-Darling (b) Murrumbidgee (c) Lachlan (d) Flinders

936. What is the largest city in New Zealand?

(a) Auckland (b) Wellington (c) Christchurch (d) Dunedin

937. What is the northernmost group of islands in French Polynesia?

(a) Tuamotu (b) Marquesas (c) Tubuai (d) Line

938. Who are the "original" settlers of Norfolk Island?

(a) Convicts from the U.K. (b) Early emigrants from Australia (c) Descendants of the mutineers of *The Bounty* (d) Americans from New England

939. What separates Australia and Papua New Guinea?

(a) Timor Sea (b) Arafura Sea (c) Coral Sea (d) The Torres Strait

940. What is the capital of Hawaii?

(a) Molokai (b) Honolulu (c) Hilo (d) Lanai

941. Which countries are separated by the Tasman Sea?

(a) Australia and New Zealand (b) Papua New Guinea and Solomon Islands (c) New Zealand and Tonga (d) Australia and New Caledonia

942. What is the political status of the Hawaiian Islands?

(a) They are independent (b) They are one of the US Trust Territories (c) They are one of the states of the USA (d) They are a US-sponsored Commonwealth

943. By what name are the original inhabitants of New Zealand called?

(a) Melanesians (b) Aborigines (c) Polynesians (d) Maoris

944. Of what territory is Rarotonga a part?

(a) Western Samoa (b) Cook Islands (c) Society Islands (d) Loyalty Islands

945. Where exactly are the Southern Alps?

(a) South Island, New Zealand (b) Northern Antarctica (c) Tasmania (d) South Australia

946. Where exactly is the Republic of Palau (Belau)?

(a) In the Hawaiian Islands (b) Next to Guam (c) In the western part of the US Trust Territory of the Pacific Islands (d) East of the Marshall Islands

947. On which island is the capital of New Zealand?

(a) South Island (b) North Island (c) Stewart Island (d) D'Urville Island

948. What separates Western Australia and the nearest Asian territory?

(a) Indian Ocean (b) Coral Sea (c) Arafura Sea (d) Timor Sea

949. What precious stone is South Australia famous for?

(a) Opal (b) Emerald (c) Moonstone (d) Sapphire

950. Of which country or territory are the Loyalty Islands a part?

(a) New Hebrides (b) New Caledonia (c) New Zealand (d) Papua New Guinea

951. Where is the Gulf of Carpentaria?

(a) Southern Papua Guinea (b) Southern Australia (c) Northwest New Zealand (d) Northern Australia

952. Society, Marquesas, Tuamotu and Tubuai are four island groups. Together, what are they known as?

(a) French Polynesia (b) Kiribati (c) Tuvalu (d) Bismarck Archipelago

953. What is Australia's most important sugarcane growing state?

(a) Northern Territory (b) Western Australia (c) Queensland (d) Does not grow in Australia

954. In what state does the River Murray flow out to sea?

(a) New South Wales (b) South Australia (c) Victoria (d) Western Australia

955. What is the capital of Papua New Guinea?

(a) Lae (b) Madang (c) Rabaul (d) Port Moresby

956. What is Mount Isa famous for?

(a) Mining (b) Opals (c) Granite (d) Sheep farming

957. Which Pacific nation has a population that is in the majority Indian?

(a) Tonga (b) Fiji (c) Western Samoa (d) Nauru

958. What is the main town of the island of Hawaii?

(a) Honolulu (b) Molokai (c) Hilo (d) Pearl City

959. What is the largest livestock population in New Zealand?

(a) Sheep (b) Cattle (c) Poultry (d) Horses

960. Where in Australia is the Great Dividing Range?

(a) West (b) South (c) North (d) East

961. In what country are the Gilbert Islands the main group?

(a) Tuvalu (b) Kiribati (c) Vanuatu (d) Tonga

962. Near what point on some maps would you find the name Amundsen, Scott and Byrd?

(a) Stewart Island (b) Queen Maud Land (c) The South Pole (d) In the Tasman Sea

963. Which is the biggest of the New Zealand islands in area?

(a) South Island (b) North Island (c) Stewart Island (d) Great Barrier Island

964. Where is Australia's Gold Coast?

(a) Near Perth (b) Near Sydney (c) Near Melbourne (d) Near Brisbane

965. What is the capital of French Polynesia and where is it?

(a) Rapa on Bora Bora (b) Papeete on Tahiti (c) Gambier in the Tubuai Islands (d) Marquesa on Papetee Island

966. In which Pacific territory is Bikini Atoll?

(a) The Marianas (b) The Caroline Islands (c) The Marshall Islands (d) The Loyalty Islands

967. On what island is Rabaul?

(a) New Britain (b) Guadalcanal (c) New Ireland (d) New Caledonia

968. What is the northernmost physical feature of the Australian mainland?

(a) Thursday Island (b) Cape York (c) Arnhem Land (d) Cape Talbot

969. Which part of Antarctica is under New Zealand's jurisdiction?

(a) Queen Mary Land (b) Victoria Land (c) Wilkes Land (d) Ross Dependency

970. Of which country is Apia the capital?

(a) American Samoa (b) Tonga (c) Western Samoa (d) Wallis and Futuna

971. Two major physical features of Australia are often considered continuations of one another. One is the Great Barrier Reef. What is the other?

(a) The Great Dividing Range (b) Cape York Peninsula (c) The Darling Downs (d) The Cumberlands and Northumberland Islands

972. Which country is disputing Britain's claim to the greater portion of the British Antarctic Territory?

(a) Argentina (b) Australia (c) Chile (d) New Zealand

973. Which country calls its districts "Statistical Areas"?

(a) Australia (b) New Zealand (c) Papua New Guinea (d) New Caledonia

974. Which Australian territories lie in the Indian Ocean?

(a) Cocos and Christmas Islands (b) Timor and Aru Islands (c) Groote and Wellesley Islands (d) Lord Howe and Norfolk Islands

975. Which two coastal towns are connected by the great north-south Australian Highway? (For its southern end, name the first town it touches on the southern coast.)

(a) Tennant Creek; Brisbane (b) Cairns; Orbost (c) Darwin; Port Augusta (d) Port Hedland; Albany

976. On which island is the capital of the Solomon Islands?

(a) Agana on Guam (b) Honiara on Guadalcanal (c) Suva on Viti Levu (d) Nuku'alofa in the Tongatapu Group

977. To which island territory did the New Zealand-administered Tokelau Islands belong till 1926?

(a) The British Gilbert and Ellice Islands (b) French Wallis and Futuna (c) French Polynesia (d) Western Samoa

978. To which semi-autonomous territory does Tinian belong?

(a) Marshall Islands (b) Palau Island (Belau) (c) The Northern Marianas (d) The Caroline Islands

979. What and where exactly is Alice Springs?

(a) A perennial spring in the Gibson Desert (b) A hot water spring in South Island, New Zealand (c) A waterfall in Australia (d) A town right in the centre of Australia

980. What was Western Australia's main mining wealth until recent years?

(a) Coal (b) Gold (c) Iron Ore (d) Silver

981. To which does Wake Island belong?

(a) The USA (b) Japan (c) Tuvalu (d) New Zealand

982. The island of New Guinea is shared by two countries. Which countries?

(a) Indonesia and Australia (b) Indonesia and Papua New Guinea (c) Papua New Guinea and the Solomons (d) Papua New Guinea and the US Trust Territory

983. To which do Wallis and Futuna belong?

(a) New Zealand (b) Fiji (c) France (d) Tonga

984. What is New Zealand's northernmost administrative centre?

(a) Auckland (b) Kaitaia (c) Wellington (d) Whangarei

985. Which Australian state or territory is the most crowded?

(a) Victoria (b) New South Wales (c) South Australia (d) Queensland

986. Which administers the Trust Territory of the Pacific Island?

(a) New Zealand (b) Australia (c) The U.N. (d) The USA

987. Which country is sometimes called the Friendly Islands?

(a) Western Samoa (b) Tonga (c) Fiji (d) Tuvalu

988. What is the sea east of Queensland where Australia has several territorial possessions?

(a) Tasman Sea (b) Pacific Ocean (c) Coral Sea (d) Arafura Sea

989. Which is the largest lake in Australia?

(a) Lake Eyre (b) Lake Torrens (c) Lake Mackay (d) Lake Moore

990. What is the major mineral resource of New Caledonia?

(a) Bauxite (b) Iron Ore (c) Phosphate (d) Nickel

991. To which do the easternmost islands in Polynesia belong?

(a) Kiribati — Flint (b) U.K. — Pitcairn (c) France — Gambier (d) New Zealand — Cook

992. Of which country or territory are the Phoenix Islands a part?

(a) French Polynesia (b) Tuvalu (c) Kiribati (d) American Samoa

993. What is the capital of South Australia?

(a) Adelaide (b) Port Augusta (c) Ballarat (d) Melbourne

994. All but three of the eleven Line Islands are part of one country. To whom do the three belong?

(a) France (b) Tuvalu (c) New Zealand (d) USA

995. Which part of New Zealand gets the heaviest annual rainfall?

(a) The northern tip of North Island (b) The southern part of South Island's west coast (c) The Banks Peninsula, South Island, (d) The east coast of North Island

996. Where exactly is Lake Disappointment?

(a) In the centre of Western Australia (b) In the Northern Territory of Australia (c) In South Australia (d) In Cape York Peninsula, Australia

997. What is New Zealand's southernmost major city?

(a) Dunedin (b) Wellington (c) Invercargill (d) Christchurch

998. Exactly how far north do Australian boundary claims extend?

(a) To islands off the coast of Indonesia's Irian Jaya (b) To islands off the coast of Timor (c) To islands off the Solomon Islands (d) To islands just off the coast of Papua New Guinea

999. What is the chief town of Guam?

(a) Agana (b) Saipan (c) Kolonia (d) Yap

1000. Besides the countries mentioned in this chapter, which other country/countries has/have dependencies in or by the island nations of the Pacific?

(a) Spain (b) Japan and Chile (c) Peru and China (d) The USSR

BONUS
EURASIA TODAY

With the map of Eurasia having changed so comprehensively since the questions for this Geography quiz book were compiled, there is no way I can get away with the footnote I added in my introduction. I therefore add these 100 questions, specifically on the new countries (or the countries in the making), as a bonus to the thousand already asked. As these supplementary questions on Eurasia are being compiled, Yugoslavia has fragmented into republics, some of whose status is none too clear, and it has been officially announced that Czechoslovakia is considering dividing itself in September 1992. These aspects of the Eurasian political situation have been taken into consideration — and accomplished to an extent — in these questions.

1. Russia is the largest in area of the countries which were part of the former USSR. What is the second largest?

    (a) Ukraine (b) Belarus (c) Kazakhstan
    (d) Kyrgyzstan

2. Which was the smallest in area of the federal units that comprised pre-1991 Yugoslavia?

    (a) Bosnia (b) Montenegro (c) Macedonia
    (d) Slovenia

3. When Czechoslovakia divides into the Czech Republic and Slovakia, what will be the capital of the smaller country?

(a) Kosice (b) Banska Bystrica (c) Zilina
(d) Bratislava

4. What is the main port of Ukraine?

   (a) Sevastopol (b) Odessa (c) Zhdanov
   (d) Kerch

5. Bohemia will be a major part of the Czech Republic when it comes into existence. What will be the other major part?

   (a) Moravia (b) Silesia (c) Ruthenia (d) Praha

6. What is Leningrad now called?

   (a) Petrograd (b) Petragrad (c) St Petersburg
   (d) Petrovesk

7. What is the capital of Croatia?

   (a) Zagreb (b) Split (c) Karlovac (d) Osijek

8. Approximately what is the area of Russia, the largest country in the world?

   (a) 11 million sq.km. (b) 17 million sq.km.
   (c) 9 million sq.km. (d) 19 million sq.km.

9. What are the highest mountains in Slovakia?

   (a) Slovakia Ore Mountains (b) Little Carpathians (c) White Mountains (d) The Tatra Ranges

10. Which country separates Croatia and the Czech Republic?

    (a) Hungary (b) Germany (c) Austria
    (d) Romania

11. Which federal unit in the 'New Yugoslavia' is called Crna Gora?

    (a) Bosnia (b) Montenegro (c) Macedonia
    (d) Serbia

12. Which autonomous region is being fought over by Armenia and Azerbaijan?

(a) Georgia (b) Dagestan (c) Kalmykstan (d) Nagorno-Karabagh

13. Which autonomous province of the 'New Yugoslavia' has a majority Albanian population?

    (a) Kosovo (b) Vojvodina (c) Nis (d) Herzegovina

14. How many autonomous republics are there in Russia?

    (a) 34 (b) 11 (c) 16 (d) 22

15. What will be the capital of the Czech Republic?

    (a) Prague (b) Brno (c) Ostrava (d) Pilsen

16. What were Armenia, Azerbaijan and Georgia called when the USSR was formed in 1922?

    (a) Transylvanian Republic (b) Transcaucasian Republic (c) Armenian Republic (d) Caspian Republic

17. Which important port town which was once a part of Slovenia is now a part of Italy?

    (a) Venice (b) Pula (c) Rijeka (d) Trieste

18. What is the main Romanian-speaking part of Moldova called?

    (a) Bessarabia (b) Transylvania (c) Wallachia (d) Dobrogea

19. Which country's name echoes the name of a Greek *nomoi* (province, or prefecture) and, as a consequence, is not getting international recognition till it changes its name?

    (a) Albania (b) Serbia (c) Macedonia (d) Bosnia

20. What is the White Russian Republic called?

    (a) Ukraine (b) Belarus (c) Moldova (d) Ruthenia

21. What is the capital of Solvenia?

(a) Ljubljana (b) Kranj (c) Maribor (d) Rijeka

22. How many countries are members of the Commonwealth of Independent States?

    (a) 13 (b) 16 (c) 3 (d) 11

23. What is Beograd generally known as?

    (a) Titograd (b) Belgrade (c) Petrovgrad (d) Novi Sad

24. Outside Prague, what is the most important industrial city in the Czech Republic?

    (a) Brno (b) Pilsen (c) Karlovy Vary (d) Ostrava

25. What substantial minority population does the Vojvodina Autonomous Province in the 'New Yugoslavia' have?

    (a) Romanian (b) Slovak (c) Hungarian (d) Bulgarian

26. What major water body is shared by Kazakhstan and Uzbekistan?

    (a) Lake Balkash (b) Aral Sea (c) Caspian Sea (d) Ural River

27. Which of the Russian autonomous republics is the largest in area?

    (a) Buriat (b) Komi (c) Tuva (d) Yakustak

28. In which country, formerly a part of the pre-1991 Yugoslavia, are there important iron mines?

    (a) Croatia (b) Slovenia (c) Bosnia (d) Serbia

29. What is the capital of Moldova?

    (a) Lvov (b) Kishniev (c) Tiraspol (d) Chernovtsky

30. What is the capital of Bosnia?

(a) Sarajevo (b) Mostar (c) Tuzla
(d) Dubrovinik

31. What river makes Bratislava a port?

(a) Elbe (b) Drava (c) Danube (d) Dneister

32. What is the capital of Montenegro?

(a) Titograd (Podgorica) (b) Kotor (c) Dubrovinik (d) Bitolj

33. Which nation with a Baltic Sea coast does Ukraine border?

(a) Latvia (b) Lithuania (c) Poland (d) Estonia

34. Which sea washes the Dalmatian Coast?

(a) Aegean Sea (b) Adriatic Sea (c) Mediterranean Sea (d) Tyrrhenian Sea

35. Which of these countries does *not* border Belarus?

(a) Estonia (b) Latvia (c) Poland (d) Lithuania

36. Which country does Armenia split?

(a) Iran (b) Turkey (c) Azerbaijan (d) Georgia

37. What was Vizhniy Novgorod known as?

(a) Kirov (b) Volgorad (c) Kalinin (d) Gorki

38. Which sea do Russia and Ukraine sandwich?

(a) Azov (b) Black (c) Caspian (d) Marmara

39. With which country does Romania have a western border?

(a) Bulgaria (b) The 'New Yugoslavia' (c) Moldova (d) Slovakia

40. To which country does the Crimea belong?

(a) Ukraine (b) Russia (c) Georgia
(d) Moldova

41. What is the capital of Belarus?

(a) Brest (b) Gomel (c) Mensk (d) Grodno

42. On which sea is the port of Murmansk?

(a) Barents Sea (b) Kara Sea (c) White Sea
(d) Norwegian Sea

43. In which country is Communism Peak?

    (a) Kazakhstan (b) Uzbekistan (c) Tajikistan
    (d) Turkmenistan

44. How big is the Czech Republic compared to
    the Slovak Republic?

    (a) Same size (b) Double the size (c) Half the
    size (d) Three times

45. Which country, formerly part of the USSR, is
    the smallest in area?

    (a) Armenia (b) Georgia (c) Moldova
    (d) Estonia

46. What is the chief mineral of the Czech Republic?

    (a) Iron ore (b) Coal (c) Glass sand
    (d) Graphite

47. What is Frunze, the capital of Kyrgyzstan, now
    called?

    (a) Osh (b) Dushanbe (c) Bishkek (d) Samara

48. With which country does Bosnia have an eastern
    border?

    (a) The 'New Yugoslavia' (b) Hungary
    (c) Romania (d) Albania

49. Of what country is Tbilsi the capital?

    (a) Armenia (b) Uzbekistan (c) Kyrgyzstan
    (d) Georgia

50. What are the chief mountains of Bosnia?

    (a) Transylvanian Alps (b) Dinaric Alps
    (c) Pindus Mountains (d) The Carpathians

51. What is the capital of Ukraine?

    (a) Kharkov (b) Kiev (c) Lvov (d) Sumy

52. How many of the former USSR republics are *not* members of the Commonwealth of Independent States?

(a) 5 (b) 7 (c) 3 (d) 2

53. Of the former republics of Yugoslavia, which voluntarily remains with Serbia a part of the 'New Yugoslavia'?

(a) Slovenia (b) Bosnia (c) Montenegro (d) Croatia

54. What is the Elbe called in the Czech Republic?

(a) Labe (b) Sazava (c) Vltava (d) Ohre

55. Which country, formerly part of Yugoslavia, has a coast on the Gulf of Venice?

(a) Bosnia (b) Croatia (c) Macedonia (d) Slovenia

56. What was Yekaterinburg known as previously?

(a) Gorki (b) Sverdlovsk (c) Kalinin (d) Kirov

57. With what country do Latvia and Estonia have eastern borders?

(a) Belarus (b) Lithuania (c) Ukraine (d) Russia

58. What is the chief city of the Tatars?

(a) Izhevsk (b) Ufa (c) Kazan (d) Kuybyshev

59. What mountains form Slovakia's north-eastern borders?

(a) Carpathians (b) Transylvanian Alps (c) Tatra Ranges (d) Sudeten Highlands

60. Which country does Tuva neighbour?

(a) Kazakhstan (b) Mongolia (c) China (d) Kyrgyzstan

61. What is the capital of Turkmenistan?

(a) Ashkhabad (b) Krasnovodsk (c) Tashkent
(d) Alma-Ata

62. Which country, as a republic of the USSR, grew the most cotton in the Soviet Union?

(a) Ukraine (b) Kazakhstan (c) Uzbekistan
(d) Russia

63. What is the capital of Macedonia, a part of the former Yugoslav federal republic?

(a) Skopje (b) Mostar (c) Pristina (d) Novi Sad

64. In which country is the Pamir Plateau?

(a) Uzbekistan (b) Turkmenistan (c) Tajikistan
(d) Kyrgyzstan

65. In which autonomous Russian republic is Lake Baikal?

(a) Buria (b) Tatar (c) Baskhir (d) Komi

66. Which country surrounds Bosnia on three sides?

(a) Yugoslavia (b) Slovenia (c) Croatia
(d) Macedonia

67. Which is the most industrialised of the Asian countries that were former USSR republics?

(a) Uzbekistan (b) Kazakhstan (c) Turkmenistan (d) Kyrgyzstan

68. Which is the only "million city" in the former Czechoslovakia?

(a) Bratislava (b) Brno (c) Ostrava (d) Prague

69. Where are the Kirgiz Steppes?

(a) Kyrgyzstan (b) Russia (c) Kazakhstan
(d) Uzbekistan

70. Which of the former USSR republics has the largest oil fields and where?

(a) Baku, Azerbaijan (b) Saratov, Russia
(c) Kuybyshev, Russia (d) Batumi, Georgia

71. What is Ust-Kamenogorsk in Kazakhstan famous for?

(a) Iron mining (b) Uranium mining
(c) Atomic ore industry (d) Natural gas

72. Which country amongst the former USSR republics has a large population of yaks?

(a) Kyrgyzstan (b) Kazakhstan (c) Uzbekistan
(d) Turkmenistan

73. From which place in Russia is there as oil pipeline to Bratislava?

(a) Moscow (b) Kuybyshev (c) Saratov
(d) Novgorod

74. In which country is the Kola Peninsula?

(a) Estonia (b) Finland (c) Lithuania
(d) Russia

75. Turkmenistan and Kazakhstan have shores on which water body?

(a) Aral Sea (b) Lake Balkash (c) Caspian Sea
(d) The Volga

76. Which is the most widely cultivated farm crop in what was Czechoslovakia?

(a) Barley (b) Sugar-beet (c) Wheat
(d) Potatoes

77. In which country does the Volga flow out to the sea?

(a) Russia (b) Kazakhstan (c) Ukraine (d) Moldova

78. Which country in the Commonwealth of Independent States has more than half the copper, lead and zinc in the whole of it?

(a) Kyrgyzstan (b) Uzbekistan (c) Kazakhstan (d) Tajikistan

79. With which country does the Czech Republic share the Sudeten Highlands?

(a) Poland (b) Hungary (c) Austria (d) Germany

80. On which river is Belgrade?

(a) Tisa (b) Drina (c) Sava (d) Drava

81. What separates Estonia from Finland?

(a) Gulf of Bothnia (b) Gulf of Finland (c) Baltic Sea (d) Gulf of Riga

82. Where is Lake Sevan?

(a) Russia (b) Georgia (c) Azerbaijan (d) Armenia

83. With which country does Slovenia share its western border?

(a) Hungary (b) Italy (c) Austria (d) Slovakia

84. Where is the Bohemian Forest?

(a) Slovenia (b) Croatia (c) Slovakia (d) Czech Republic

85. From which country does the River Prut separate Romania?

(a) Russia (b) Moldova (c) Hungary (d) Bulgaria

86. Tilsit was an important town in East Prussia which Russia absorbed in 1946. What is it now called?

(a) Sovetsk (b) Kaliningrad (c) Kaunas (d) Grodno

87. Which sea does the Gulf of Ob join?

(a) Laptev Sea (b) East Siberian Sea (c) Kara Sea (d) Barents Sea

88. From which country did the Karelian Autonomous Republic acquire additional territory in 1940?

(a) Germany (b) Finland (c) Poland (d) Estonia

89. Into which country do the Balkan Mountains extend from Serbia?

(a) Bulgaria (b) Macedonia (c) Bosnia (d) Romania

90. What was the *lingua franca* of the 1945 Republic of Yugoslavia?

(a) Slovene (b) Macedonian (c) Serbo-Croat (d) Serbian

91. What is Kazakhstan's best known livestock?

(a) Cattle (b) Goats (c) Pigs (d) Sheep

92. Which is the Ukraine's main river?

(a) Dniester (b) Dnieper (c) Bug (d) Don

93. Which Baltic nation, formerly part of the USSR, has a capital which is not a port?

(a) Estonia (b) Russia (c) Latvia (d) Lithuania

94. What is the capital of Kazakhstan?

(a) Alma-Ata (b) Uralsk (c) Taskhent (d) Samarkand

95. Which country has the largest port on the Caspian Sea?

(a) Russia (b) Azerbaijan (c) Kazakhstan (d) Armenia

96. To which country does Novaya Zemlya belong?

(a) Lithuania (b) Estonia (c) Latvia (d) Russia

97. What is the major 'New Yugoslavia' junction from which trains go to Bulgaria and Greece?

(a) Belgrade (b) Nis (c) Skopje (d) Pec

98. With which country does the Danube form one of Slovakia's borders?

(a) Czech Republic (b) Austria (c) Hungary (d) 'New Yugoslavia'

99. Which part of Moldova wants to secede because the major part of the country has Romanian links?

(a) Trans-Dneister (b) Trans-Prut (c) Bessarabia (d) Ukrainian Moldova

100. How many new countries (including Russia) has the break-up of the USSR added to Europe?

(a) 12 (b) 6 (c) 10 (d) 9

ANSWERS

GENERAL GEOGRAPHY

1.(c)	2.(b)	3.(b)	4.(a)	5.(d)
6.(b)	7.(c)	8.(b)	9.(a)	10.(d)
11.(c)	12.(a)	13.(a)	14.(b)	15.(d)
16.(a)	17.(c)	18.(a)	19.(c)	20.(b)
21.(d)	22.(b)	23.(c)	24.(b)	25.(d)
26.(c)	27.(d)	28.(a)	29.(d)	30.(a)
31.(a)	32.(c)	33.(d)	34.(a)	35.(b)
36.(d)	37.(a)	38.(b)	39.(c)	40.(a)
41.(b)	42.(d)	43.(d)	44.(b)	45.(a)
46.(a)	47.(b)	48.(a)	49.(a)	50.(c)
51.(d)	52.(b)	53.(a)	54.(c)	55.(d)
56.(b)	57.(a)	58.(b)	59.(a)	60.(c)
61.(d)	62.(a)	63.(b)	64.(d)	65.(a)
66.(b)	67.(d)	68.(b)	69.(d)	70.(a)
71.(c)	72.(d)	73.(a)	74.(b)	75.(d)
76.(a)	77.(d)	78.(a)	79.(b)	80.(c)
81.(b)	82.(a)	83.(d)	84.(a)	85.(c)
86.(d)	87.(a)	88.(b)	89.(c)	90.(a)
91.(b)	92.(c)	93.(d)	94.(b)	95.(b)
96.(c)	97.(d)	98.(a)	99.(d)	100.(a)

NORTH INDIA

101.(b)	102.(a)	103.(c)	104.(d)	105.(b)
106.(c)	107.(a)	108.(b)	109.(c)	110.(d)

111.(a)	112.(b)	113.(d)	114.(c)	115.(a)
116.(b)	117.(c)	118.(d)	119.(a)	120.(b)
121.(a)	122.(c)	123.(d)	124.(a)	125.(c)
126.(b)	127.(c)	128.(a)	129.(b)	130.(c)
131.(a)	132.(d)	133.(b)	134.(a)	135.(d)
136.(c)	137.(a)	138.(d)	139.(b)	140.(a)
141.(c)	142.(d)	143.(a)	144.(a)	145.(b)
146.(d)	147.(b)	148.(a)	149.(c)	150.(d)

SOUTH INDIA

151.(b)	152.(a)	153.(c)	154.(d)	155.(b)
156.(a)	157.(d)	158.(c)	159.(b)	160.(a)
161.(b)	162.(d)	163.(c)	164.(a)	165.(b)
166.(c)	167.(d)	168.(a)	169.(b)	170.(d)
171.(a)	172.(c)	173.(b)	174.(d)	175.(b)
176.(a)	177.(c)	178.(d)	179.(b)	180.(a)
181.(b)	182.(c)	183.(d)	184.(c)	185.(a)
186.(b)	187.(d)	188.(a)	189.(c)	190.(b)
191.(d)	192.(a)	193.(c)	194.(b)	195.(a)
196.(c)	197.(d)	198.(b)	199.(d)	200.(a)

EAST INDIA

201.(c)	202.(a)	203.(d)	204.(b)	205.(b)
206.(c)	207.(c)	208.(a)	209.(c)	210.(d)
211.(a)	212.(b)	213.(c)	214.(b)	215.(a)
216.(d)	217.(a)	218.(c)	219.(b)	220.(d)
221.(a)	222.(c)	223.(b)	224.(a)	225.(b)
226.(a)	227.(c)	228.(b)	229.(d)	230.(c)
231.(d)	232.(a)	233.(b)	234.(c)	235.(d)
236.(a)	237.(b)	238.(d)	239.(c)	240.(b)
241.(a)	242.(d)	243.(c)	244.(b)	245.(a)

246.(a)   247.(d)   248.(b)   249.(c)   250.(a)

WEST AND CENTRAL INDIA

251.(d)   252.(a)   253.(b)   254.(c)   255.(a)
256.(d)   257.(a)   258.(b)   259.(c)   260.(a)
261.(d)   262.(b)   263.(c)   264.(a)   265.(a)
266.(d)   267.(b)   268.(a)   269.(a)   270.(b)
271.(c)   272.(d)   273.(c)   274.(a)   275.(b)
276.(d)   277.(a)   278.(b)   279.(d)   280.(c)
281.(b)   282.(a)   283.(d)   284.(c)   285.(a)
286.(b)   287.(d)   288.(c)   289.(b)   290.(a)
291.(b)   292.(c)   293.(a)   294.(d)   295.(b)
296.(d)   297.(c)   298.(b)   299.(a)   300.(c)

SOUTH ASIA

301.(a)   302.(c)   303.(d)   304.(a)   305.(b)
306.(d)   307.(c)   308.(a)   309.(b)   310.(c)
311.(a)   312.(c)   313.(d)   314.(a)   315.(c)
316.(b)   317.(a)   318.(c)   319.(d)   320.(a)
321.(b)   322.(c)   323.(a)   324.(b)   325.(c)
326.(d)   327.(b)   328.(d)   329.(a)   330.(c)
331.(d)   332.(a)   333.(b)   334.(c)   335.(a)
336.(b)   337.(d)   338.(c)   339.(a)   340.(a)
341.(d)   342.(a)   343.(c)   344.(b)   345.(b)
346.(c)   347.(a)   348.(d)   349.(a)   350.(b)
351.(d)   352.(a)   353.(c)   354.(b)   355.(d)
356.(a)   357.(b)   358.(c)   359.(d)   360.(a)
361.(b)   362.(c)   363.(d)   364.(a)   365.(c)
366.(b)   367.(d)   368.(a)   369.(b)   370.(d)
371.(b)   372.(c)   373.(a)   374.(b)   375.(d)
376.(b)   377.(a)   378.(c)   379.(d)   380.(c)

381.(a)	382.(c)	383.(d)	384.(b)	385.(c)
386.(a)	387.(b)	388.(d)	389.(c)	390.(a)
391.(b)	392.(c)	393.(a)	394.(b)	395.(d)
396.(c)	397.(d)	398.(a)	399.(b)	400.(b)

THE REST OF ASIA

401.(b)	402.(a)	403.(d)	404.(c)	405.(a)
406.(b)	407.(d)	408.(a)	409.(b)	410.(a)
411.(d)	412.(c)	413.(a)	414.(b)	415.(c)
416.(d)	417.(a)	418.(b)	419.(c)	420.(a)
421.(b)	422.(a)	423.(d)	424.(c)	425.(c)
426.(a)	427.(b)	428.(c)	429.(a)	430.(b)
431.(c)	432.(d)	433.(a)	434.(d)	435.(b)
436.(a)	437.(d)	438.(a)	439.(c)	440.(c)
441.(a)	442.(b)	443.(c)	444.(d)	445.(a)
446.(b)	447.(c)	448.(d)	449.(a)	450.(d)
451.(c)	452.(a)	453.(b)	454.(d)	455.(a)
456.(c)	457.(b)	458.(c)	459.(b)	460.(a)
461.(d)	462.(a)	463.(c)	464.(b)	465.(d)
466.(a)	467.(b)	468.(a)	469.(b)	470.(c)
471.(b)	472.(d)	473.(a)	474.(b)	475.(c)
476.(a)	477.(b)	478.(d)	479.(a)	480.(b)
481.(c)	482.(d)	483.(a)	484.(b)	485.(c)
486.(a)	487.(b)	488.(d)	489.(c)	490.(a)
491.(b)	492.(a)	493.(d)	494.(a)	495.(c)
496.(d)	497.(a)	498.(b)	499.(c)	500.(b)

AFRICA

501.(d)	502.(a)	503.(b)	504.(c)	505.(a)
506.(b)	507.(a)	508.(d)	509.(b)	510.(c)
511.(a)	512.(b)	513.(a)	514.(d)	515.(c)

516.(a)	517.(b)	518.(d)	519.(c)	520.(a)
521.(b)	522.(c)	523.(d)	524.(a)	525.(b)
526.(c)	527.(d)	528.(a)	529.(b)	530.(c)
531.(d)	532.(a)	533.(b)	534.(d)	535.(a)
536.(c)	537.(b)	538.(a)	539.(c)	540.(d)
541.(b)	542.(c)	543.(a)	544.(b)	545.(d)
546.(a)	547.(a)	548.(c)	549.(d)	550.(a)
551.(b)	552.(c)	553.(a)	554.(d)	555.(b)
556.(a)	557.(b)	558.(c)	559.(d)	560.(a)
561.(b)	562.(a)	563.(d)	564.(c)	565.(a)
566.(b)	567.(a)	568.(b)	569.(d)	570.(c)
571.(a)	572.(b)	573.(c)	574.(b)	575.(d)
576.(a)	577.(b)	578.(c)	579.(a)	580.(b)
581.(c)	582.(d)	583.(a)	584.(b)	585.(c)
586.(d)	587.(a)	588.(c)	589.(b)	590.(d)
591.(a)	592.(b)	593.(c)	594.(a)	595.(b)
596.(d)	597.(a)	598.(b)	599.(c)	600.(d)

EUROPE

601.(b)	602.(b)	603.(c)	604.(b)	605.(d)
606.(a)	607.(b)	608.(a)	609.(c)	610.(d)
611.(b)	612.(a)	613.(c)	614.(c)	615.(a)
616.(d)	617.(b)	618.(c)	619.(a)	620.(b)
621.(d)	622.(a)	623.(c)	624.(d)	625.(a)
626.(b)	627.(c)	628.(d)	629.(c)	630.(a)
631.(b)	632.(d)	633.(c)	634.(a)	635.(d)
636.(a)	637.(b)	638.(c)	639.(b)	640.(b)
641.(d)	642.(b)	643.(c)	644.(a)	645.(a)
646.(c)	647.(d)	648.(a)	649.(b)	650.(a)
651.(c)	652.(a)	653.(b)	654.(c)	655.(d)
656.(a)	657.(b)	658.(c)	659.(a)	660.(d)

661.(a)	662.(b)	663.(d)	664.(b)	665.(a)
666.(d)	667.(c)	668.(d)	669.(b)	670.(a)
671.(c)	672.(d)	673.(b)	674.(a)	675.(b)
676.(a)	677.(d)	678.(b)	679.(c)	680.(a)
681.(b)	682.(d)	683.(b)	684.(a)	685.(b)
686.(c)	687.(b)	688.(d)	689.(a)	690.(b)
691.(a)	692.(c)	693.(b)	694.(d)	695.(a)
696.(b)	697.(d)	698.(a)	699.(c)	700.(b)

NORTH AMERICA

701.(c)	702.(a)	703.(d)	704.(b)	705.(d)
706.(a)	707.(c)	708.(a)	709.(b)	710.(c)
711.(d)	712.(a)	713.(b)	714.(c)	715.(a)
716.(d)	717.(b)	718.(c)	719.(d)	720.(a)
721.(b)	722.(c)	723.(d)	724.(a)	725.(b)
726.(a)	727.(d)	728.(b)	729.(a)	730.(c)
731.(b)	732.(d)	733.(a)	734.(c)	735.(b)
736.(a)	737.(b)	738.(c)	739.(d)	740.(a)
741.(c)	742.(b)	743.(d)	744.(c)	745.(a)
746.(b)	747.(a)	748.(c)	749.(d)	750.(a)
751.(b)	752.(c)	753.(a)	754.(d)	755.(b)
756.(a)	757.(c)	758.(b)	759.(d)	760.(a)
761.(d)	762.(a)	763.(b)	764.(c)	765.(b)
766.(a)	767.(b)	768.(a)	769.(b)	770.(c)
771.(d)	772.(b)	773.(a)	774.(c)	775.(a)
776.(b)	777.(c)	778.(d)	779.(a)	780.(d)
781.(b)	782.(c)	783.(a)	784.(b)	785.(d)
786.(a)	787.(c)	788.(a)	789.(d)	790.(b)
791.(c)	792.(a)	793.(d)	794.(b)	795.(a)
796.(c)	797.(b)	798.(d)	799.(a)	800.(c)

SOUTH AMERICA

801.(b)	802.(a)	803.(c)	804.(d)	805.(a)
806.(b)	807.(c)	808.(d)	809.(a)	810.(c)
811.(b)	812.(a)	813.(d)	814.(c)	815.(a)
816.(b)	817.(c)	818.(d)	819.(b)	820.(a)
821.(b)	822.(c)	823.(a)	824.(d)	825.(c)
826.(a)	827.(b)	828.(d)	829.(c)	830.(a)
831.(b)	832.(d)	833.(c)	834.(a)	835.(c)
836.(a)	837.(b)	838.(d)	839.(c)	840.(a)
841.(b)	842.(c)	843.(a)	844.(d)	845.(a)
846.(b)	847.(c)	848.(a)	849.(b)	850.(d)
851.(a)	852.(c)	853.(b)	854.(d)	855.(a)
856.(b)	857.(c)	858.(a)	859.(b)	860.(a)
861.(c)	862.(b)	863.(d)	864.(a)	865.(d)
866.(b)	867.(a)	868.(d)	869.(a)	870.(b)
871.(a)	872.(c)	873.(d)	874.(a)	875.(b)
876.(c)	877.(d)	878.(b)	879.(a)	880.(c)
881.(d)	882.(b)	883.(a)	884.(c)	885.(d)
886.(a)	887.(b)	888.(c)	889.(a)	890.(d)
891.(b)	892.(a)	893.(c)	894.(d)	895.(b)
896.(a)	897.(c)	898.(d)	899.(b)	900.(a)

AUSTRALASIA AND ANTARCTICA

901.(d)	902.(a)	903.(b)	904.(a)	905.(c)
906.(d)	907.(a)	908.(b)	909.(c)	910.(d)
911.(a)	912.(b)	913.(c)	914.(a)	915.(d)
916.(b)	917.(a)	918.(c)	919.(b)	920.(d)
921.(a)	922.(b)	923.(d)	924.(c)	925.(a)
926.(b)	927.(a)	928.(c)	929.(b)	930.(c)
931.(a)	932.(d)	933.(b)	934.(c)	935.(a)

936.(a)	937.(b)	938.(c)	939.(d)	940.(b)
941.(a)	942.(c)	943.(d)	944.(b)	945.(a)
946.(c)	947.(b)	948.(c)	949.(a)	950.(b)
951.(d)	952.(a)	953.(c)	954.(b)	955.(d)
956.(a)	957.(b)	958.(c)	959.(a)	960.(d)
961.(b)	962.(c)	963.(a)	964.(d)	965.(b)
966.(c)	967.(a)	968.(a)	969.(d)	970.(c)
971.(a)	972.(c)	973.(b)	974.(a)	975.(c)
976.(b)	977.(a)	978.(c)	979.(d)	980.(b)
981.(a)	982.(b)	983.(c)	984.(d)	985.(a)
986.(d)	987.(b)	988.(c)	989.(a)	990.(d)
991.(b)	992.(c)	993.(a)	994.(d)	995.(b)
996.(a)	997.(c)	998.(d)	999.(a)	1000(b)

BONUS: EURASIA TODAY

1.(c)	2.(b)	3.(d)	4.(b)	5.(a)
6.(c)	7.(a)	8.(b)	9.(d)	10.(c)
11.(b)	12.(d)	13.(a)	14.(c)	15.(a)
16.(b)	17.(d)	18.(a)	19.(c)	20.(b)
21.(a)	22.(d)	23.(b)	24.(a)	25.(c)
26.(b)	27.(d)	28.(c)	29.(b)	30.(a)
31.(c)	32.(a)	33.(c)	34.(b)	35.(a)
36.(c)	37.(d)	38.(a)	39.(b)	40.(a)
41.(c)	42.(a)	43.(c)	44.(b)	45.(a)
46.(b)	47.(c)	48.(a)	49.(d)	50.(b)
51.(b)	52.(a)	53.(c)	54.(a)	55.(d)
56.(b)	57.(d)	58.(c)	59.(a)	60.(b)
61.(a)	62.(c)	63.(a)	64.(c)	65.(a)
66.(c)	67.(b)	68.(d)	69.(c)	70.(b)
71.(c)	72.(a)	73.(b)	74.(d)	75.(c)
76.(b)	77.(a)	78.(c)	79.(a)	80.(c)

81.(b)	82.(d)	83.(b)	84.(d)	85.(b)
86.(a)	87.(c)	88.(b)	89.(a)	90.(c)
91.(d)	92.(b)	93.(d)	94.(a)	95.(b)
96.(d)	97.(b)	98.(c)	99.(a)	100.(c)

REFERENCES

1. The George Philip's range of atlases.
2. The John Bartholomew range of atlases.
3. *The Statesman Year-Book 1988-89.*
4. *The Hammond Almanac.*
5. *The World* — A General Geography by Sir Dudley Stamp (Orient Longman).
6. *The Survey of India School Atlas.*
7. *The Manorama Year Book 1989.*
8. *The Traveller's Companion* (TT. MAPS).